Martha Remick

Millicent Halford

A Tale of the Dark Days of Kentucky in the Year 1861

Martha Remick

Millicent Halford
A Tale of the Dark Days of Kentucky in the Year 1861

ISBN/EAN: 9783743422438

Manufactured in Europe, USA, Canada, Australia, Japa

Cover: Foto ©Andreas Hilbeck / pixelio.de

Manufactured and distributed by brebook publishing software (www.brebook.com)

Martha Remick

Millicent Halford

A TALE OF THE

DARK DAYS OF KENTUCKY

IN THE YEAR 1861.

BY MARTHA REMICK,

AUTHOR OF "AGNES STANHOPE."

"There's a divinity that shapes our ends,
Rough-hew them how we will."

BOSTON:
A. WILLIAMS & CO., 100 WASHINGTON STREET.
1865.

INNES AND NILES,
Stereotypers and Printers,
37 CORNHILL.

INTRODUCTION.

THE following pages record the history of a Kentucky family — not very unlike in its experiences to those of a thousand others — through the first year of the war just ended, and in the few months which preceded its breaking out. Care has been taken to render the narrative as veritable as circumstances would permit, and to lean as little from the far New England stand-point as early prejudices would allow. Slowly before us the terrible drama opened. God sealed our eyes in the beginning, because of our participation in the state of things which warmed it to life; but the dullest heart must acknowledge at last that, though his vengeance sleep for a hundred years, his ear is never closed to the cry of redress for wrong. His hour has come. From him are the issues closing before us to the happy end.

CONTENTS.

———•••———

v

Millicent Halford.

CHAPTER I.

THE LETTER.

IN the autumn of 1860, a young girl, Millicent Halford, left her New England home, located in a quiet village town of Massachusetts, to become an inmate of her aunt's family in Kentucky. The circumstances of this adoption on the one side were unusually sorrowful. By the death of her father, the young girl had found herself bereft of her nearest friend and only protector. Her step-mother, a widow at the period of her marriage, with a large family of children, and scanty means, was not likely to take much interest in her prospects.

"I don't know what you will set about, Milly," said bustling, energetic Mrs. Halford, when the first days of mourning had worn away, and the family began to turn their attention to the future. "You might have learned a dressmaker's trade, as I suggested last spring, if your father hadn't been so proud. What's the use of bringing a child up in idleness, I'd like to know? or what good is all the schooling you've had at the Academy going to do you?"

"I might teach," said Millicent, forcing down a sigh, suggested perhaps by a glimpse of the pale, sickly face and slender figure which confronted her opposite in the mirror, or by the cold, unsympathizing tones of her step-mother. "You know that was father's thought."

"And where are you to get a school, Milly?"

"I don't know, ma'am, I'm sure."

"I don't know, either," said Mrs. Halford, shortly. "If your father had listened to me, he would have given you a trade."

"I have not got an answer to my letter to Aunt Leeson," observed Millicent, hesitatingly. "Perhaps she will suggest something; she can guess how we are circumstanced. I dare say she could get me a place to teach. If I were only competent, I might be a governess."

"*She* wont help you much," said Mrs. Halford, dryly. "I doubt if she answers your letter at all."

Millicent's eyes filled with tears. The same doubt had arisen in her mind only the past night, when, for the third time, she had turned away disappointed from the steps of the village post-office. Her aunt had never liked her (Millicent's) mother's marriage with simple Farmer Halford, and a broken and irregular correspondence was all the intimacy which had been kept up between them after that event to the date of the younger sister's death. Then Mrs. Leeson's letters had entirely ceased, and no communication had taken place between the families until Millicent's letter, which her father had, as his last parting words, when she knelt by his dying-bed, desired her to write. No doubt, poor man! he had a distinct idea of the lonely and rugged life to which he was leaving her.

"A letter to-night, Milly!" said James, the eldest boy, a fine lad of fifteen, coming in from the driving rain-storm which was splashing great drops outside the window, and swelling the already swollen gutters in the road.

Milly took it eagerly, her cheeks flushing with a fever of surprise and pleasure.

"It's from Aunt Leeson," she said, looking at the postmark, and proceeding to tear it open.

"Well, what does she say?" asked Mrs. Halford, after what seemed to her a lengthened delay on the part of her step-daughter.

"She invites me to come to live with her, and says she shall be glad of my services to teach her little girl."

Mrs. Halford looked relieved; she was glad to get her step-daughter off her hands.

"It's a good offer," she said, "and there is no reason why you should not accept it."

Certainly there was not. Mrs. Halford moved away to the oven to tend the cakes which were doing to a fine brown in its depths, and Millicent began to lay the coarse but snowy cloth on the round table for tea. Presently she stole up-stairs to her little chamber, and dropping into her low chair by the window, pored again by the dim twilight over the few lines in her aunt's letter. They were coldly traced,—not a word of that sympathy for which her heart went out in passionate yearning in her late bereavement. Mrs. Leeson wrote in the stereotyped tones of duty, and plainly thought that she was accomplishing some great charity in offering a home, however burdened with conditions, to her orphan niece.

"I wonder if she will like me," thought Milly, gazing, in a mirror of memory, at her pale, plain face and shy, retiring ways. "I'm afraid she wont. Now if it had been Fanny—"

Fanny was her step-mother's daughter, a rosy-cheeked, merry girl of just her own years, — fresh seventeen, — but as unlike her in all outward appearance as could well be.

"Milly!" said a voice at the foot of the staircase.

The girl started up at her mother's voice, and ran down. The biscuits were smoking upon the table, and Mrs. Halford was in the act of pouring out the tea. Milly took her place next to James. A new subject was coming up in her thoughts. What would her aunt say to her wardrobe? It was slender and of modest materials. She had an idea that her aunt would desire her to make a better appearance.

"When do you set out, Milly?" asked her step-mother at the close of the meal. "I suppose Mrs. Leeson is to send on for you. You never could find the way there by yourself; it's hundreds of miles."

"She said her eldest son, ma'am, was in New York, and I could meet him there."

"But how are you to get to New York,

I'd like to know? You never have set your foot beyond Boston yet, and your father wouldn't have trusted you to go alone."

"No doubt we can think of a way," said Milly, quietly. "There is Mr. Carden, who will be going on, or sending some one, for goods; he would take charge of me, perhaps."

"Most likely he's gone before this; it's the middle of September now."

"Perhaps not, ma'am. I'll write him a note to-night, anyhow."

"When is your cousin to be there?"

"He is in New York now, Aunt Leeson says, and will remain there until I join him."

Little more was said. Millicent washed up the supper things, and retired to her chamber, this time with a lamp, to write her note. She had no very bright anticipations of the future as she folded it up and sat in a little fit of musing, while the rain sobbed drearily outside the window, and pattered heavily upon the roof overhead. She was about to quit her home,

the only home she had ever known, in all
probability never to return to it. True, she
had experienced little of affection or sympathy in it in these later years; but each
low, dark room held its pictures of days
that were gone. Even the old gnarled apple-trees outside, the clump of lilacs, and
the little garden which every June had
seen flushed with pinks and sweet-williams
were dear. The future looked very sad
to the young girl, vista after vista opening
out into the distance as she sent her
thoughts into the years. What did it hold
for her? Why was she about to be trans-
planted into new scenes so far from this
dear spot?

She heard Fanny's cheerful voice in the
entry; she was in the act of ascending the
staircase, and her mother's answering tones
rose behind her. Milly hurried to put out
her light, and crept into bed. In that frugal household, it would have been judged
a grave impropriety to meditate by lamp-
light. Her step-mother had supposed her in
bed an hour before.

CHAPTER II.

THE JOURNEY.

MILLICENT'S note met a favorable answer. Mr. Carden had been detained by illness in his family from setting out on his visit to New York at the usual date, and cheerfully promised the protection of his escort to the young lady. She had little time for preparation, as he was to start on the day but one following. Her trunk was hastily packed. There was no time, had the means been in her possession, for attempting an improvement in her wardrobe; and, with an exchange of trembling good-bys, she took her seat in the stage which was to carry her on the first few miles of her journey. She had taken her leave of her step-mother in the house; her

2   17

brothers and sister were grouped on the steps to see her off.

"I wish I were going too, Milly," said Fanny, in an undertone, thinking more of the excitements and novelties of the journey than the strange faces that waited at the end. "You'll be sure to write to us,—wont you?—and tell us all about the place when you get there?"

"I shall miss you about my arithmetic, Milly," said James, a suspicious moisture shining up in his honest brown eyes. "I sha'n't have anybody to show me about my sums the long fall evenings."

"Good-by," said Milly again, sinking back into her corner of the stage. The driver pulled up his reins, and the horses started on at a jogging pace. Soon they were past the pear-tree which flung its long arms over the bend of the road, had crossed the bridge lined with willows, passed the red schoolhouse, the meeting-house, with its tall spire, a long row of scattering farmhouses, and Millicent drew her head in wearily from the contemplation of new sights and unfamiliar spots. The green fields were yet sprinkled with the white frost of the past night, which had crisped the edges of many a long row of bean-vines, and withered whole gardens of blossoms.

The ride began to grow long to Millicent before the railway station was reached, where the stage-driver kindly helped her on board the cars, which had drawn up almost at the same moment with the appearance of the stage. Soon the train started off with voluminous floods of smoke, keeping its way through the open country.

It was quite dusk in the short autumn day when the puffing engine slackened its speed within sight of a row of red brick walls rising over the outskirts of a wide marsh, and Millicent knew that the train was approaching the end of its journey. Presently it glided into a long, dark building, passing the windows, framed with the faces of passengers, of a waiting train, and came to a halt

Melicent, following the general movement, found herself outside in the din and confusion of a crowd of vociferous hack-drivers. Searching in her port-monnaie for Mr. Carden's card, she was soon in a carriage, and in a few moments alighted at the end of a substantial brick block, in a quiet street near the depot. She had been here once before with her father, on the occasion of one of his short visits to town, and a very kind welcome met her from the pleasant, motherly-looking woman whom the abrupt pull at the bell brought to the door to receive her.

"You look tired, my dear," said Mrs. Carden, showing her guest into her parlor, and assisting her to remove her bonnet and shawl. "How early did you leave home?"

"The stage started at eight, ma'am."

"You must be hungry as well as tired. Did you get a luncheon on the way?"

"No, ma'am. I had no appetite."

"Well, tea will be ready soon; Mr. Car-

den comes in at six. I have just told
Jane to make up the fire. My husband
tells me you are going a long journey."

" Yes, ma'am."

" Going to be a governess, I believe Mr.
Carden said ? "

" No, ma'am," — Millicent colored slightly.
Was it a false feeling? — "I'm going to live
with my aunt."

Why did Mrs. Carden's eyes rest upon
the homely but serviceable shawl which she
was folding upon her arm, in the act of
taking it up-stairs, and the plain silk bonnet, which should have been crape? or did
Millicent only imagine this?

" I suppose your aunt is very wealthy,"
she said, hesitating; "has lots of slaves.
People do mostly, I've been told, in Kentucky."

" I don't know," said Millicent. "Father
used to say Aunt Leeson was rich; but
I have never seen her, and we had no
letters from her after mother died until this
one came."

"How long has your mother been dead?"

"Eight years." Millicent's voice dropped to a subdued tone.

"A long time." Mrs. Carden finished folding the shawl over her arm, and taking the bonnet in her hand, went up the staircase.

"How I wish I could have some nicer clothes!" thought Millicent, taking a chair by the window. "I'm afraid Aunt Leeson wont be pleased with me. But how could I help it? Where was the money to come from?"

Her father had left very little except the small farm, which he had conveyed to her step-mother by his will for the support of his two youngest children. She had had her plain suit of mourning with Fanny. What had she to complain of?

There was very little to see on the street outside; the red brick walls shut out the sky, and besides, the twilight was beginning to fall.

Presently a key grated in the street

door. Mr. Carden had let himself in, and his steps died away down to the lower regions, in which a bell presently sounded, and Mrs. Carden made her appearance to show her guest down to the basement dining-room, where the tea-table was spread.

"We must be ready betimes in the morning, Miss Halford," said Mr. Carden, as Millicent, confessing to fatigue, quitted the family group at an early hour after tea; "the express train goes out at nine."

CHAPTER III.

THE KENTUCKIAN FAMILY.

WE will precede Millicent to the little Kentuckian household of which she is about to become a member. It consists of Mrs. Leeson, the mistress; her two sons, the elder of whom is now absent on a visit to New York (Millicent's escort), the younger at present at home on a stay of a few days snatched from the close study of his profession in the office of an eminent lawyer at Bowling Green; her little daughter of twelve; her husband's orphan niece, Miss Augusta Leeson, and some twelve or thirteen servants, the latter varying in complexion from the deepest tint of ebony to a rich quadroon. Miss Augusta Leeson is not, however, a permanent

24

inmate of this home; she has arrived here quite suddenly on a visit, and inopportunely in the absence of her *fiancé*, Mr. Frederick Leeson.

It may as well be confessed in the commencement that this match has been hardly of the young couple's framing. Interested friends, the mother, and the young lady's guardian have used their interest to bring about the engagement, and though the affair promises well on the surface, and the marriage is settled to come off in the spring, on the lady's side, at least, it has very little of the coloring of affection.

"I must tell Jim to drive over to the depot for Frederick," observed Mrs. Leeson on the afternoon of her son's expected arrival, as she sauntered out on the lawn with her niece. "Adéle has gone up to her chamber with a headache. Poor child! I wonder how she will like her new teacher. She is so hard upon governesses. I don't suppose the girl will have much appearance, brought up as she has. been in an out-of-the-way Yankee town."

Mrs. Leeson had certainly forgotten that she was once herself a Yankee girl, born and bred in a quiet New England village, married to a poor clerk, who, by some lucky strokes of fortune, became a wealthy merchant, as whose widow she had been honored with the hand of the Kentucky gentleman who had become her second husband, leaving her, after a short and not very happy marriage, a second time a widow.

"You said Miss Halford was very young, I think," observed Miss Leeson, in reply to her aunt's speech.

"Yes, barely seventeen. I wish she had been a year or two older." Mrs. Leeson stooped to gather some of the late roses which blew in thick clusters in a sheltered spot against the garden-wall. "Her letter is very prettily written though; she claims to have had a tolerable education, and even a smattering of French and Latin— Jim!" she raised her voice suddenly to catch the ear of the coach-boy, a tall, ebony-colored youth of twenty, who was lounging lazily in the sun outside the stable buildings, "harness up the horses and drive over to the station. Your master, Frederick, comes in the afternoon train."

"Yes, missis." The boy jerked off his cap, and replacing it on his woolly head, started at a quick pace to the stable-yard.

"These lazy niggers," said Mrs. Leeson, turning to a fresh subject of conversation, "they don't half of them earn their bread. They need a right smart overseer. That grain crop ought to have been reaped in these fine days. This is the fourth day they have been at work upon it; but they'll do next to nothing while Fred. is away; he's too easy with them."

"Why don't you manage in his absence?" asked Miss Leeson.

"Why, what would be the use? His plans of governing and mine don't agree. We agreed that I was to have the ordering of the house-servants, and he the out-of-door hands. That was the understanding when he came of age. Fred. is as easy a master as ever lived, — too much so for his own interests."

Mrs. Leeson had got to the end of her walk, and, with her hands full of roses, began to retrace her steps up to the house. She went into the large, open sitting-room, whose windows opened on a balcony, or veranda, running the length of that side of the house, while her niece, separating from her at the door, sauntered on to an orchard of apple-trees which lay a little to the left, quite within range of view from the windows.

Perhaps the beauty of the day, the mild, warm air, and the soft sunshine lured the young lady under these friendly shadows which spread above an emerald carpet. It was quite impossible she could have distinguished the tall, stationary figure which held a position in the background.

"Augusta!"

Miss Leeson gave a pretty little start of surprise as Mr. James Leeson quitted

the fence against which his back had
been placed, and came up to her side,
holding out his hand half-entreatingly for
one of the late summer roses she was
drawing absently through her fingers.

"Will you give me one of these flowers for a keepsake? I am going away this
evening."

"So soon!" The color flushed up faintly
into the young lady's cheeks. It might
have been from the surprise, the request,
or it might have · had its origin in quite
another source of emotion.

"Yes, it is quite three days over the
time fixed upon for my stay,"—Mr. James
possessed himself quietly of the coveted
flower, which he was audacious enough to
take to his lips, — "and there is no reason
why I should linger. Frederick will be
here to-night."

"I shall miss you," said Augusta, dropping her eyes, and the quiet fading out
of the glow in her cheek did not indicate
much pleasure in the greeting of her expected bridegroom.

Mr. James did not take advantage of the reply, if any advantage could have been taken. Perhaps he caught at the instant a glimpse of his mother, who had taken her chair at one of the low French windows opening on the veranda, an observation which was taken at the same moment by his cousin. It was not desirable to the young people to be seen in apparently confidential conversation in the apple-orchard. Miss Augusta gathered up the remnant of her flowers, and Mr. James, transferring his purloined rosebud to his vest-pocket, accompanied her up the walk to the house.

Mrs. Leeson made no opposition to her son's announcement of departure. She had, in fact, been expecting it for a day or two, and had experienced some disquiet over a state of affairs which was as plain to her quick perceptions as it must have been to those of any other interested looker-on. Miss Leeson was certainly allowing herself to forget the relations which she held to Frederick as his affianced wife, and

James was surrendering himself with inexcusable weakness to a strong passion for his future sister-in-law.

"Frederick's coming will make all right," thought the anxious mother, with a sigh of relief, resuming her sewing which, for the last few moments, had dropped idly against her knee, while Augusta languidly turned the leaves of a fresh book upon the table, and Mr. James sauntered back again into the open air. Neither of the three was happy or quite at ease. Mrs. Leeson could not crush down a consciousness that she had not acted quite rightly in bringing about this engagement, weighty as were the considerations that hung upon it. Mr. James's natural sense of honor reproached him as having been grievously in error in yielding weakly to his unexpected temptation, and winning away the affections of his brother's betrothed. Augusta, she had a dismal consciousness that Mr. Frederick's appearance was to take place that night, and that she was expected to get up a show of gladness at his coming.

CHAPTER IV.

THE RECEPTION.

MR. FREDERICK LEESON'S carriage was at the station, drawn up a few paces from the platform, when that gentleman emerged from the train, pausing to assist, with scrupulous politeness, in the descent of his travelling companion, a little slender, plainly-attired girl, whom Jim's rolling eyes at once recognized as the expected Yankee teacher.

"All well at home, Jim?" asked Mr. Leeson, leisurely helping his cousin into the vehicle, and preparing to follow her, while the boy, who had sprung down from his perch, proceeded to lift up the trunk and valise to their places.

"Yes, mass'r." Jim's eyes brightened

32

with the consciousness of a valuable piece
of information. "Miss Augusta, sir, have
come down on a visit, and Mass'r James
be at home too."

"Ah!" Mr. Frederick's face expressed
satisfaction. Plainly he was not yet in
the secret of his lady-love's fickleness. He
had by this time taken his place in the
carriage. Jim, having accomplished the
strapping of the trunk and valise, climbed
up on his perch; the reins were drawn
in, and the horses started off at a good
pace.

Millicent leaned on her cushion, much
too wearied with the fatigue of her unac-
customed journey to look out at the scen-
ery through which she was passing, — the
pretty level grain-fields, the scattered houses,
with their clusters of barns and gray out-
buildings, the hills stretching away in the
distance.

Presently the carriage turned off from
the road, and rolled up a broad green avenue opening to the front of a house, which

3

seemed to be composed of a collection of buildings, with a wide veranda running round the western side.

Jim pulled in his reins at the door. Mr. Leeson alighted, and assisted Millicent from the carriage. A handsome woman, with silver threads just shining in her black hair, which she wore without a widow's cap, came out into the hall as they stepped in, followed by a young lady attired with much elegance.

Millicent shrunk back a little to give place to the first greeting which passed between the son and his mother; but her part immediately followed.

"You seem very tired, Millicent," said Mrs. Leeson, giving her her hand. "My niece, Miss Augusta Leeson. I will call Dinah to show you up to your chamber. Tea will be ready in half an hour."

Millicent was glad of the dismissal, and followed the negress, who, with a showy red bandanna bound round her head, preceded her up the staircase to the room appropriated to her use. It was small, quite apart from the commodious guest-chambers and the rooms occupied by the family; but two narrow windows looked out on a pleasant interval of country. Dinah, Mrs. Leeson's special waiting-maid, threw a glance around the room, to see that the ewer was filled with water, and everything in its place.

Millicent began to take off her bonnet and bathe her face, and, after some little hesitation, asked that her trunk might be brought up. She wished to make a more presentable appearance before her aunt than her dusty travelling dress would admit.

Dinah went out, and, in a few moments, the trunk made its appearance, and selecting a muslin dress and fresh collar, she hastened to finish her toilet. It was hardly completed when the supper-bell rang, and Dinah reappeared to show her the way to the dining-room.

The family were already seated at the

table. Mrs. Leeson directed Millicent to a seat beside her daughter, who eyed her new governess with critical attention.

Little was said to Millicent during the repast. Mr. Frederick Leeson addressed to her one or two observations, making himself generally agreeable, like the thorough gentleman that he was. Miss Augusta quite ignored her presence. (Mr. James was not present, having, as it proved, started away on the same train by which his brother had arrived.)

If Millicent had entertained any romantic ideas of the reception which awaited her, they must, by the end of that long half-hour, have been completely put to flight. She saw and felt that her position in her aunt's family was to be simply that of a hired governess, without, perhaps, any exact statement of wages.

"When did you quit home, Millicent?" asked Mrs. Leeson as, supper over, the family withdrew into the sitting-room.

"A week ago, ma'am."

"So Frederick kept you waiting a day or two in New York?"

"Yes, ma'am; he was not quite ready to start."

"Your letter missed me, mother," observed the gentleman from his distant seat at the open window. "I did not get it till the morning I took the train."

"It was Jim's carelessness in neglecting to post it, I haven't a doubt," said the lady, emphatically; "it's just like him. I will look into it to-morrow."

Augusta laid down a book, the leaves of which she had been turning carelessly under the blaze of the astral, as her cousin addressed some observation to her. The young lady's face wore a clouded expression. She was suffering with a headache, she said, and Mr. Frederick's sympathy was expressed with much feeling.

"You may retire, Millicent, if you wish," observed Mrs. Leeson, noticing the young girl's air of weariness. "A night's rest will put you up after your journey. You

will find a lamp, if you can penetrate to
the kitchen."

Millicent said "Good-night," and thank-
fully accepted her dismissal. A clear, full
moon was shining out of doors, and she
had no hesitation in seeking her way up
to her chamber without the doubtful search
into the servants' regions. The moonlight
shimmered brightly through the open curtains over the white counterpane of the
bed and the cheap gray carpet, knotted
here and there on its surface with a
pretty group of flowers.

Millicent took her Bible from her trunk,
and after an ineffectual attempt to distinguish a few lines, closed the book, and surrendered herself to a fit of meditation. She
felt the strangeness of the place, and the
sense of loneliness which surrounded her.
In her child days, she had been taught
that an overruling Providence directs the
events of every life; and the lesson learned
at her mother's knee had always been
treasured up.

CHAPTER V.

FIRST IMPRESSIONS.

MILLICENT did not wake until late on the following morning. A night of sound sleep had succeeded the fatigues of her journey. The sun was shining brightly upon her pillow when she opened her eyes, and with a sense of the lateness of the hour, hastened to rise. The air was sweet as she threw up her window and leaned out for an instant in the pause between the conclusion of her simple toilet and the act of emerging from her chamber. As she did so, her ear caught a sound which seemed to be the stifled cry of a human being in distress, and which appeared to proceed from the cluster of out-buildings abutting to the left of her window.

39

"Somebody is in distress," thought Millicent, anxiously.

The opening of the door caused her to draw her head in. A bright-looking mulatto girl, whom she had seen waiting on the table the past night, stood in the opening.

"Something is the matter, Rose," she said, hurriedly. "Somebody is hurt. Come here and listen!"

"It's only Jim, Miss Halford," said the girl, her eyes dilating with a curious expression. "He went and done forgot to post missus' letter to Mass'r Frederick, and she's having him whipped for it."

Millicent shuddered. It was inhuman, cruel! The color came up hot into her face.

"Missus sent me up to tell you it is 'most breakfast-time," said the girl, preparing to go out; "the bell rings in ten minutes."

Millicent went back to listen at the window. The muffled cries had ceased. Jim's punishment was ended.

Mrs. Leeson received Millicent, when she descended to the breakfast-room, with rather more kindness than she had done on the previous night, and even expressed a hope that she had rested well. Miss Leeson bade her a languid good-morning, which was repeated with more animation by Mr. Frederick on his entrance, and Adéle came running in from the garden, her lap full of fragrant flowers. It was a pleasant picture, — the breakfast-table, with its snowy damask covering, its glistening . china, its fresh rolls, and amber-hued coffee; the yellow canaries singing cheèrily in their cage in the window; the bright, warm sunshine irradiating every corner. But a shadow lay over it all, — Millicent heard, in fancy, the cry which had startled her in her chamber.

"I had Jim whipped this morning for forgetting your letter," observed Mrs. Leeson toward the close of the nearly-silent repast. "I'll warrant he wont forget a thing of this kind again in a hurry."

Adéle raised her eyes suddenly from her plate to her mother's face. Mr. Frederick's brow contracted with a careless mixture of disapproval and indifference. Miss Leeson did not regard the matter as of sufficient importance to attract her attention.

"It's time that grain crop was got in," said Mrs. Leeson, as a general movement was made to quit the table. "The hands have been at it for a week. It's over-ripe, and if a heavy rain should come upon it, it would beat it out."

"I shall see to it to-day," said her son; "there's plenty of time. Augusta, what are your plans for the morning? Will you drive, or a ride on horseback? If the last, I shall be happy to be your cavalier."

"I have a new book commenced which I am interested to see the end of," replied the young lady, turning her face a little aside to the window.

"Adéle will show you up to her schoolroom," said Mrs. Leeson, speaking rather shortly to Millicent. "Come, my dear, give those flowers to Rose; she will dispose of them in the vases."

"I don't want to be shut up in the schoolroom, mamma, this bright morning," pouted Adéle. "It will be sure to bring back my headache puzzling over those musty books."

"Show Millicent up-stairs," said Mrs. Leeson, reaching forward to take the flowers out of her daughter's hand. "Do as I bid you!"

Adéle sulkily obeyed, and preceded her cousin up the staircase. The schoolroom was in an eastern angle of the house; the door opening into it adjoined Millicent's chamber. It was a large, airy apartment, well furnished with maps, charts, and cases of books. A portfolio of drawings lay on a table in a distant corner. One of them had slipped to the floor. Adéle went forward and picked it up.

"Do you draw, Miss Halford?" she inquired, a faint glow of interest brightening up her sullen mood. "I like to paint; but I hate this dull grammar and algebra."

"A little," said Millicent, taking the drawings from her hand to look them over. "Are these sketches yours?"

The fine touch displayed in them might well have elicited the surprised question.

"No, not mine. I can't begin to do anything like that. They are Fred.'s."

"Sketches of landscapes in this vicinity, I suppose?" hazarded Millicent, laying them down. "This last is exquisite," still holding it in her hand. "This wood and water, — I have seen them before. Where?"

She could not tell why a quick shudder came over her, and the healthy blood faded out of her cheek. Are there such things as premonitions? Had she seen it in her dreams?

"That is a Virginia landscape," said Adéle, looking at her troubled face with curious surprise. "Most of these pictures are. Frederick sketched them last spring, when he was at Tudor Hall."

Millicent restored it to its place in the portfolio, and commenced examining her pupil, to ascertain the extent of her acquirements. If she had feared that her young cousin was already too far advanced to derive much benefit from her instructions, she was soon agreeably disappointed, and quite surprised, by the lamentable ignorance that met her researches.

"We will take these French verbs this morning," she said, marking off the first lesson; "and these exercises in algebra are to follow."

Adéle seated herself with a dismal resignation in her corner, and Millicent took up a stray volume of poems which had found its way up from the sitting-room table.

"If I can only make her love me," she thought, glancing at the momentarily-absorbed child, "I shall not feel quite alone."

Could she?

CHAPTER VI

AUNT PHILLIS' SICKNESS.

GLAD were both teacher and pupil when the long morning finally came to an end, and the dinner-bell summoned them to the lower regions. Adéle had blundered through her French verbs, and came to a determined stop over her second tough problem in algebra. Still the patience and gentleness of her new teacher were not wholly thrown away. She did not scold her, like odious Madame Marchet, or threaten, like sour Miss Lindsley, to report her dulness and inattention to mamma.

The afternoon was at Millicent's disposal, and, on leaving the dining-room, a few steps behind her aunt, she sauntered out on the lawn in front of the house, and

46

after exploring the garden, turned into a
path which led off in the direction of the
kitchen and out-buildings. The windows of
the first were open. A slender, wearied-
looking woman was standing at her iron-
ing-table, which she had placed in a position to take advantage of the little fresh
air which was stirring. A little child, of
a year or more, was playing in the doorway. Both the mother and child were
white, the former with only the faintest
traces of mulatto blood in her rich complexion.

Millicent stopped to speak to the child,
and accepted the chair which the woman
left her work to place for her.

"I've been so hurried to-day!" said the
laundress. "Mistress expected me to get
this done an hour ago; but what with this
troublesome child and Aunt Phillis to tend
upon, I couldn't. Baby's good now though,"
glancing at the child, rolled up in a ball
on the doorstep, "and aunty will have to
wait awhile for her cup of balm tea."

Millicent glanced at the pitcher of herbs
steeping upon the stove, struck by the
last observation, and hesitated to offer her
services. The woman eyed her with some
curiosity, looking up from her steady process of smoothing the muslins, a large pile
of which still lay damp upon the table.
It was her first sight of the new governess.

"It will take you some time to finish
yet," observed Millicent presently. "Shall I
take the tea up to the sick woman? I
have nothing to do."

"Thank you very kindly, Miss Halford,"
said the woman, proceeding at once to
pour it out, — "if 'tisn't too much trouble.
Phillis' chamber is up them stairs, the second door to the right. She's down sick,
poor aunty! Got a fever on her, I think,
and worry of mind too." The last sentence she added in a lowered voice, half
to herself.

Millicent took up the bowl of medicine,
and proceeded as well as she could up

the steep stairway. She knocked at the
door.

"Come in," said a feeble voice, and
raising the latch, she found herself in a
small chamber, lighted by a narrow window, the open sash of which afforded a
very imperfect ventilation, besides letting
an unhealthy draught directly upon the
head of the straw pallet, which, with a
chair and small table, constituted the furniture. An aged negress, her brow wrinkled with furrows, and her short hair
blanched to a grizzly white, lay on the
bed, and sent a restless glance toward the
door as it opened.

"Laws, miss, you needn't hab taken de
pains," she said, as Millicent poured out a
part of the tea in a cup which stood on
the table, and bent over the bed. "I can
drink widout being helped."

"You seem very feverish," remarked her
visitor, conquering her repugnance to sit
down in the vacant chair, which she saw
plainly, in the wistful eyes watching her,
she was expected to do.

"Yes, dear, I's bery sick." She lay back with a groan.

Millicent debated in her mind the propriety of closing the window and opening the door. The latter would afford better ventilation. To leave both open, with the full air beginning to stir out of doors, would hazard too powerful a draught. The sick woman groaned again.

"You seem very ill," said Millicent, gently. "Have you had a doctor?"

"No, chile. Missus was in last night, and she didn't tink it necessary. She said to Susan, gib me plenty ob balm tea. But I's worse to-day. It's all 'bout Jim, miss. 'Pears like I can't keep him out ob my mind."

Millicent remembered the little event of the morning, which had thrown such a shadow over her spirits upon her first introduction to her new home.

The old woman hesitated to open her troubles to the Yankee governess; but Millicent's sympathizing looks, with the light-

headedness of fever, which was beginning
to impart a restless hurry to her spirits,
loosened her tongue.

"It's all 'bout Jim's being whipped, miss;
he aint used to it. I's worrying what'll
come ob it. Missus don't know him; he's
a smart, bright boy; but he wont be good
for anyting now de whip's been used; he's
jes' like what his farder was."

"Is Jim your grandson?" asked Millicent, less from curiosity than a loss what
to say.

"Yes, dear, and he's all I's got left to
me in de worl'. Missus bought him when
she bought me; dat's a good many years
ago. He was a little bright pickaninny
of ten, and I was a smart, strong woman.
'Pears like I's 'most got through my labors now."

"Is your son living?" asked Millicent.

"I dunno, dear. He was sold down in
Georgia 'fore I came here. I b'longed to
Mas'r Rhet, and Harry did too. It nearly
tore my heart out to part wid him, de

boy, and see him go off in de driver's gang; but one poor comfort, he couldn't fare worse dan he had. Mas'r's oberseer used to beat him cruelly."

"Miss Halford," said Adéle, putting her head into the chamber, "mamma wants to speak to you."

The girl's face expressed much wonder at her governess' occupation, as Millicent, putting the cup which she held in her hand on the table, rose to follow her down the staircase.

"I have looked all over the house for you," said Adéle, "till Susan told me you were with Aunt Phillis."

The laundress was still at work on the muslins as they crossed the kitchen. The pile showed little diminution.

Mrs. Leeson was in the sitting-room, sewing at one of the open windows.

"Can you do fine sewing, Millicent?" she asked, as her niece joined her.

"Yes, ma'am, very well."

"Perhaps you will assist me then over

this," rising to get her basket, which stood on the table.

Millicent accepted the offered work, and drew her chair at a respectful distance from her aunt's.

Adéle inquired for her cousin. Augusta had gone out to drive with Frederick, Mrs. Leeson replied, with an air of satisfaction; they had taken a long distance, to some spot she mentioned, and would probably not be at home before nightfall.

Adéle pouted slightly. She would have liked to share this pleasure.

"Miss Halford has been up with Aunt Phillis, mamma," she said presently. "I found her in her room. Aunty looks really sick."

Mrs. Leeson threw a quick, dissatisfied glance at her niece.

"If Phillis gets worse, I must send for a doctor," she said. "I saw nothing alarming when I visited her last night. The balm tea she is taking will check the fever."

"I guess aunty worries about Jim's being whipped," said Adéle. "Rose said she was quite out of her head this morning."

"Pshaw!" said her mother. "The boy needed it before this; he'd have got it, too, if he had had a right smart master, instead of a woman, to train him. He will have a better memory for it, after he gets out of his sullenness."

He *was* sullen then. Millicent bent lower over her sewing. Every word of her aunt seemed to bring to her a throb of pain. The young girl had heard in her distant New England home of a race of people who were bought and sold like dumb beasts in the market; but the story had floated past her like an idle tale. Now she found herself standing on the threshold of these scenes of wretchedness and misery.

CHAPTER VII.

THE MORTGAGE.

IF Mr. James Leeson had improved his brother's absence to lay suit to his betrothed, during his accidental visit to his home in the beginning of her stay, the lost ground seemed, to all outward appearance, to be pretty effectually recovered by Mr. Frederick. Augusta's headache passed off with the evening of his arrival; the interesting book which had detained her indoors from the pleasure of a tête-à-tête drive with her lover was finished in the course of the morning, and at the suppertable the young lady presented a face as smiling and rosy as it was ever her wont to wear. Only one present guessed that she had had a hard struggle with herself,

55

and had come off, for the time, at least, con-
queror. No doubt, the manner of her parting with Mr. James had helped in her
newly-formed decision. The gentleman had
taken his leave of her in the presence of
his mother, with a cool _empressement_ which
whispered no hope upon his part of an
early meeting. It had only been a flirta-
tion. Augusta had said it angrily to herself the past night upon her pillow; or,
if he really cared for her,—and words and
tones came up to keep that idea in her
mind,—his passion was not strong enough
to overleap the obstacles between them.

Mrs. Leeson was much pleased with this
favorable turn of affairs: but a doubt was
beginning to cross her mind as to the ex-
pediency of delaying this marriage six
months, which would bring round the end
of April, the time fixed upon for the wedding. Augusta had demurred at May, with
the old English prejudice that it was an
ill-omened month for a bridal. A looker-on
might have doubted if this marriage would

prove fruitful of happiness under any circumstances.

Mrs. Leeson, like the wise and provident
woman that she was, took an opportunity
of breaking the subject to her son, opening it, not upon the ground which was
actually the basis of her interest, but from
quite a different point. She alluded to the
unfortunate pecuniary circumstances which
had first aroused her interest in the match,
and the partial mortgage that lay upon
her son's estate, and which would come
due by the approaching January. It was
in the dusk of twilight. The mother and
son had found a few moments alone in the
sitting-room; Augusta had just left them;
Millicent and Adéle were taking a stroll
in the garden.

Frederick colored, and made a movement
as if he would have interrupted his mother's flow of words. He really loved his
cousin in his quiet way, and though not
blind to the advantages to accrue from her
wealth in his unhappily embarrassed circum-

stances, he had much too correct a sense
of honor to have asked the hand of any
woman solely from that circumstance.

"Bennet will wait," he said, carelessly.
"He is an old neighbor, and will not be
in a hurry to foreclose the mortgage."

"I am not sure," said Mrs. Leeson, a
little uneasily. "We are old neighbors, as
you say; but the state of affairs between
us is not quite what it used to be. James
has been foolishly offering some attentions
to his daughter."

"It would be a respectable match for
him," said Frederick. "The young lady is
amiable and agreeable. My dear mother,
what objections can you have to offer?"

"I? The affair seems to be broken off.
That is the matter. Your brother James
is like most other young men,—always
caught by the last pretty face."

"Ah," said Frederick, musingly. "Well,
I don't think this will make any difference with Mr. Bennet. If it should, I
dare say I can easily raise a loan."

"Just like you," said his mother, shortly, "putting off till to-morrow everything that has the appearance of care or trouble; but why not hurry up your marriage a little? It may as well take place at New Year's as in April."

There was some propriety in the suggestion. Frederick thoughtfully considered it.

"Your engagement has lasted for a year," observed his mother. "Augusta's stay with us, she told me an hour ago, will not extend beyond the middle of November; she has promised her guardian to return by that time. Of course, you will escort her home, a favorable opportunity to ask for the shortening of your probation."

Perhaps the mother and son would not have felt quite as composed in this careless tête-à-tête, had they been aware that, in her exit, Augusta had left the door that opened behind them ajar, and for herself, had gone no farther than the wide entry, in which she loitered to enjoy the cool air from the veranda. In this position, all of her aunt's remarks reached her ears, and a portion of her cousin's replies. The embarrassed circumstances of her future husband were for the first time made known to her, and a second thought told her that her ignorance of the moment before had been fully shared by her guardian. A tumult of angry blood rushed to her temples; she stood perfectly still, to struggle with the new revelation.

"How fortunate that I do not love him!" she thought. "And I have been blaming myself for doing him injustice!"

The quick steps of Millicent and Adéle were hurrying up the walk a moment later, and the supper-bell would soon ring. She glided on tip-toe through the entry, and managed to make a noiseless ascent of the staircase, the soft carpet burying the sound of her footsteps.

Perhaps her conscience told her she had not acted rightly in listening; yet the current of air through the unclosed door had borne the conversation to her ears with the first sentence. How could she choose but listen?

CHAPTER VIII.

MRS. LEESON was at fault in supposing Phillis' sickness to be but a slight attack of fever from which a few days would see her recovered. The old woman grew much worse, and at the last point the doctor was called. He felt her pulse, examined her symptoms, and pronounced the case a hopeless one, which might terminate fatally in twenty-four hours.

Rose, the bright-faced mulatto girl, wiped away a few tears. Jim, the most interested person, heard the announcement of his grandmother's condition with the apparently sullen indifference which had characterized him since the morning of the whipping.

61

"Phillis was a good servant in her day," remarked Mrs. Leeson, coming back from her visit to the chamber; "but she had got to be so old and decrepit she had almost got through her labors; she was of little use before this attack came on;" and she dismissed the subject.

Millicent bent over her work with a pressure of uneasy thoughts. Death in the house! It wore to her a solemn appearance; she could not put it out of her reflections.

The last stitch was taken in the muslin skirt which her aunt had given her to complete. Mrs. Leeson was gone out, and Millicent, with an idle half-hour upon her hands, threaded her way out aimlessly into the kitchen. A dull, drizzling rain was falling out of doors, an unlooked-for change from the clear, bright atmosphere of the previous day. Susan was busy over some plain sewing, with her baby crawling contentedly on the floor. Lizzie, the cook, was actively kneading dough for the supper biscuit. Both looked up at Millicent's appearance. Their serious faces contrasted with the indifferent ones she had just left. Susan's eyes were suspiciously swollen.

"How is Phillis getting on?" asked Millicent, in a low voice, stepping into the room.

"Poorly, Miss Halford," said Susan, dropping her eyes. "Rose said a minute ago she was just gone. Wont you step up and see her?" she asked, rising.

Millicent hesitated; but the girl was already on the staircase, and some indefinable feeling told her she might possibly be of use in that death chamber. She had seen her father die. His calm, peaceful sinking away had divested death of much of her childish terror. She went up behind Susan with a few quickened heartbeats, and stopped at the door of the chamber.

The dying woman was quite conscious; her head lay back on the pillow, her large eyes wide open, and her hands keeping a tremulous movement on the bed-clothes. She was quite alone, Rose, who had been keeping watch with her, having just stepped out. The power of speech had not yet left her.

"Is dat you, Susan?" she asked, looking toward the door. "I's very thirsty."

Millicent gave her the cup of water that stood on the table.

"'Most ober Jordan," she whispered, in her husky voice, "de Lord be praised! It's all clear now. He'll bring Jim safe. I's not 'fraid to trust him now."

Millicent sat down in the chair, and put her handkerchief to her eyes.

"If you would please read a chapter, Miss Halford," whispered Susan, "I'm sure she would like it."

Millicent looked for the Bible.

"I will run into mistress' room and get it," said Susan, hurrying out.

"Is it possible she has no Bible of her own?" thought Millicent. She forgot, for the moment, that a knowledge of letters is supposed by their masters to place slaves above their condition. She might be pardoned in this early instance for her forgetfulness; for Susan's skin was little removed in tint from her own.

Susan came back with the handsomely-clasped volume, and Millicent, opening it, turned to that beautiful chapter of John which will be read in death chambers and sorrowing homes so long as the earth is peopled with the sorrowing and the dying. She read on, interrupted now and then by Aunt Phillis' fervent ejaculations, till the close was reached. Rose had come back, and she got up to go out.

A change had taken place in the dying woman. As, in the act of rising, she looked toward the bed, Millicent saw that her eyes were set, and the restless hands lay quite still. Rose, with the animation peculiar to her race, burst into loud sobs.

"Hush," said Susan, "hush, Rose! You'll disturb her; she's going out of all her troubles. I wish I was going too, I do!"

5

Millicent stepped out, the last words ringing painfully in her ears. What if she, too, had been born a slave, like poor Susan?

Nothing was said of the dying old servant around the supper-table. The conversation flowed on between Mrs. Leeson and her son. Augusta was moodily silent, speaking only when spoken to, and then with an apparent effort; and little was addressed to Millicent.

The evening passed much as usual. Frederick and Augusta varied its monotony by a game of chess. Adéle watched the play. Mrs. Leeson took up a book, and Millicent made a show of following her example.

A few stars were shining through the rifts of clouds when Millicent went up to her chamber. The storm, which had exhausted itself during the last hour in a torrent of rain-drops, was breaking away. She thought of poor old Phillis as she sent her gaze up into the blue depths. Almost home! The fetters of a slave about to drop from her wearied limbs! What ecs-

tatic happiness and joy waited to crown
her!

Mrs. Leeson brought a clouded face to
the breakfast-table on the following morning. Something had gone wrong. Millicent
saw that plainly in her absorbed preoccupation.

"Jim has run off," she said, relieving her
mind of the announcement toward the close
of the meal.

Frederick started, and put down the cup
which he was in the act of raising to his
lips. Augusta went on deliberately with
the process of spreading the remnant of
her roll. Adéle stopped with her toast on
her fork.

"You must be mistaken, mother!" said
Frederick. "When did you find it out?"

"A few moments ago. I wanted to send
him on an errand, and he was nowhere to
be found."

"Have you had the out-buildings examined?"

"Yes, thoroughly; his cot was not slept

in last night; he was not seen by any of
our people after the first part of the evening."

"He has got a good start," said Frederick, with a lowering brow, as he pushed
back his chair from the table. "I must
set out at once to search for him. Why
did you not tell me when you first made
the discovery?"

"A few moments will make little difference. I did not wish to interrupt breakfast. He cannot have got far on foot;
most likely he is resting now in some
woods."

"It was a dark night," observed Mr.
Leeson, rather to himself, as he turned to
go out.

Millicent heard him call to his body servant, from the next room, to get out his
horse. She sat balancing her spoon tremblingly on her cup. None of the family
had followed Mr. Leeson's hurried movement of departure from the table. If the
poor slave should be overtaken and brought

back, what would be his punishment? She felt at that moment that, if circumstances had permitted, she could have done a great deal to assist in his concealment from his master. She saw the latter ride past the window a few minutes later, in the bright sunshine, closely followed by his servant, Tom, and Mrs. Leeson at the same instant gave the signal for rising.

"Oh, how earnestly I hope he may be going on a fruitless errand!" prayed Millicent; but the dull sinking at her heart told her that her fears held more than a balance with her hopes.

CHAPTER IX.

RETURN OF THE FUGITIVE.

MR. LEESON did not make his appearance at dinner. He did not, in fact, arrive at home till near nightfall. Millicent was sitting by the open window when she saw him ride up the avenue, his mounted servant following behind him, and another figure, which she was at no loss to identify as poor Jim's, moving rapidly along at his horse's rein. This was the culmination of her feverish restlessness through the long day, of her nervous starts at the warbling of a bird, or the falling of a dead leaf. Oh, if she could only gather the courage to beg Mr. Frederick to be merciful, and for this once to let the poor fellow's offence go unpunished!

She turned to look at Miss Leeson, who had come out of the reverie which had held her through the morning, and was chatting with Adéle, who, with her lap full of roses, lingered on her way to the dining-room.

"Jim is found!" said Mrs. Leeson, suddenly opening the door. "He has led Frederick a long hunt; he will get his punishment for this, and a hard punishment too. Adéle, where is Rose? I saw her in the garden with you a minute ago."

"She went round to the kitchen, mamma, as I turned to come this way."

"Very well." She closed the door, Adéle passing out with her.

Millicent turned to Augusta, conquering the dislike which that lady's distant ways toward herself had caused, to address her.

"Miss Leeson," she said, hurriedly, "will you intercede with Mr. Frederick for poor Jim? He will have him beaten terribly for this running away, if you do not."

Augusta lifted up her eyes in extreme astonishment.

"I never interfere in such matters, Miss Halford," she replied, coldly.

"What a fool I was," thought Millicent, "to suppose she had a grain of feeling in her heart!"

It would be to no purpose to ask Adéle; she was but a child, and her entreaties would avail nothing. Her aunt she well knew to be inflexible. Her heart sank with a dumb helplessness.

The supper-bell rang shortly. Mr. Leeson made his appearance, freshened by a change of suit from the disorder of his journey, and quite in his usual even spirits.

Nothing was said of Jim until the close of the meal; then, as the movement to leave the table was made, Augusta carelessly asked her cousin, —

"Where did you find your runaway?"

"In a wood about twelve miles from here. A good night's walk he made of it. I should have been back before; but I passed the spot a long way, and then turned back and beat in all directions.

Nobody had seen him. It was merely perseverance that hunted him up."

Millicent shuddered.

"He will have time to repent his folly," said Mr. Leeson. "I have ordered him a moderate whipping, and shall keep him on bread and water for three or four days, with little of that."

"Your leniency is all thrown away," added his mother; "the boy needs a severe castigation. Nothing short of the whip will take the sullenness out of him. He'll run away again as soon as he gets a chance!"

"I don't believe in whipping," said Mr. Frederick, "only when it can't be helped, and then moderately. Mother and I seldom agree upon this point."

Miss Leeson did not give her opinion. Probably the subject possessed little interest for her. The family adjourned to the sitting-room, where Mr. Leeson's portfolio was discovered lying on the table, having made its descent in Adéle's hands from the

upper regions of the schoolroom. One or
two of the sketches proved to be new to
Augusta, and she began to turn them over.

Millicent, unnoticed by the group in the
conversation which came on, shortly quitted her corner, and stepped out through
the low, open window on the veranda.
She had at first no object in her change
of position beyond a longing to feel the
breath of the cool night air upon her fevered temples; but, mechanically, her steps
turned toward .the angle formed by the
kitchen, in the direction of the out-buildings, in one of which, out of the group,
she knew the recovered slave must be
confined. The kitchen was alight, as she
passed, and the figures within distinctly
visible. Rose was sitting at a little distance from the table, her head bent down
upon her hands; Susan was steadily sewing; Lizzie was paring a pan of apples.
She threw a glance up at the dark window of Phillis's chamber, just visible by
the light of the stars. Phillis was no

longer there; her worn-out form had been laid away that afternoon to its kindred dust in the little graveyard on the slope.

"I wonder if they know in heaven what befalls us here?" queried Millicent, as she groped her way on. She passed the carriage-house and the stable. A little farther on a low moan drew her attention. This must be the place in which Jim was confined. "How much I should like to see him and speak to him!" she thought; "but I dare not."

Another figure came gliding up, as she stood back in the shadow, and passed close to the locked door. It bore Susan's height and figure, a handkerchief closely enveloping the head.

"Jim," she said, in a low whisper, putting her mouth close to the aperture of the key-hole, — "Jim!"

"Who's dar?" asked a sullen voice inside.

"It's me, Jim, — only Susan. How do you feel to-night? I've run out to speak to

you; but I darsn't stay but a minute."
She put her ear to the key-hole. Millicent
listened intently for the answer; but none
came. "I darsn't stop," said the woman,
speaking again. "Jim, I wish I could give
you something to eat; but mistress keeps
everything locked. You must be hungry."

Jim made no answer. A slight stir on
Millicent's part rustled a dead leaf under
her dress. Susan started, and ran lightly
toward the house.

"I, too, may be missed," thought Millicent; and she judged it best to turn her
steps back to the veranda.

CHAPTER X.

SALE OF SUSAN'S HUSBAND.

POOR Jim's hungry state was the first thought that came into Millicent's mind in the morning, as she unclosed her eyes from the sound, refreshing slumbers of youth. The sun was shining brightly, and she hurried through her toilet, stopping to throw a glance out of her window at the line of out-buildings, one of which, to her quickened sight, covered a scene of wretchedness and misery. As she lingered, her eyes fell suddenly upon a group below that riveted her attention, and turned her thoughts into a fresh channel. The foremost figure was Susan, who stood with her face covered with her hands, her form apparently shaking with sobs, while close

77

beside her was a young, sturdy-looking mulatto, whose face expressed the acme of silent wretchedness. A few paces off, the baby was lying upon the wet grass, quite unnoticed by either of the couple in their preoccupation.

Millicent leaned forward, trying to comprehend the scene; but the distance prevented the words, if any were spoken, from reaching her ears. The breakfast-bell called her away. She hurried to give the finishing touches to her hair, and went down. She met Adéle coming in from the garden as she reached the foot of the staircase.

"What is the matter with Susan, Adéle?" she asked, a fear that Mrs. Leeson had discovered the girl's visit of the past night, and that it had taken place contrary to some direct orders, creeping over her.

"Mr. Bennet has sold Sam, Susan's husband," replied Adéle.

This, then, was the explanation. Millicent pitied the poor girl with all her heart.

"Why didn't your brother buy him?"

asked Millicent. "Where are they going to take him?"

"Fred. has as many negroes as he wants," said Adéle, answering the first question, with a look of surprise. "The trader who has bought him will take him off to Georgia, mamma says. The bargain is agreed upon, but isn't finished. If it was, Sam wouldn't have had liberty to come here. He found out somehow that his master was about to sell him."

Millicent went on to the breakfast-room with her charge. The fresh rolls, the dainty buckwheats, and amber-hued coffee had at no time worn a less tempting appearance. Only a stone's throw from this sunshiny apartment and these cheerful faces two poor human hearts were nearly breaking.

"Susan is in a great way about Sam this morning," remarked Mrs. Leeson, taking up one or two ordinary topics of conversation. "Mr. Bennet has sold him."

"Ah! Who is the purchaser?" asked Frederick.

"A Georgian trader, I believe, who came along a day or two ago. He has been stopping at Hildreth's, — over to the tavern. Sam found it out this morning, and ran over to tell Susan."

"It's a hard case," said Mr. Leeson, deliberately helping himself to a fresh roll. "I wouldn't part with one of my slaves on any account; I go upon principle in the matter."

Mrs. Leeson glanced at her niece's plate, the contents of which remained nearly untouched.

"You seem to have quite lost your appetite, Millicent," she said.

"I am not feeling very well, ma'am."

"A turn in the fresh air will do you good. Adéle's lessons can wait for an hour."

They were leaving the table. Millicent seized upon the permission to go out on the veranda. The morning air was cool and sweet. She wondered if Susan was still lingering by the out-buildings. A few steps farther satisfied her that the mournful parting was over. Susan was not to be seen on the spot where she had watched her from her window. She had gone in with her child.

A little later, Miss Augusta Leeson came out in her riding-dress, a pair of horses making their appearance from the stable in the care of black Joe. Her cousin assisted her into her saddle, and springing into his, the couple were soon cantering down the avenue.

"How gracefully she rides!" thought Millicent, following them with her eyes.

She went back into the house, the hour Mrs. Leeson had given her having nearly expired. She must open Adèle's lessons, however wavering the attention she might be able to fix upon them. She did not catch a glimpse of poor Susan until evening; then she found her in the kitchen to which an errand for Mrs. Leeson took her. It was a message the lady had forgotten to give her cook, and which, de-

7

tained by the sudden appearance of company, a couple of visitors from the neighborhood, she intrusted to her niece.

Susan was sitting at the table at her sewing, precisely in the same position as on the previous night; but the great change in her face from its habitually wearied expression to a sullen despair told the story of suffering beneath.

Millicent lingered when she had done her errand to Lizzie. She wondered if Susan's husband had already gone, if they had no hope of meeting again. She glanced at the child, who lay sleeping soundly on a cushion at its mother's feet.

"Sam went dis morning," whispered Lizzie, interpreting her look. "De trader took him off wid de rest."

Low as were the tones of the communication, they seemed to reach Susan in her distant corner of the room; for her work slipped from her hands, and she burst into a tempest of convulsive sobs, such as had wrung her frame in the morning.

"Now I's done de mischief!" exclaimed Lizzie, with a frightened look, the glass dish which she held in her hand slipping to the floor and parting in a dozen fragments. "Oh, what will missus say?" her eyes riveted on the pieces.

"Let her alone," said Dinah, Mrs. Leeson's maid, who had come in unobserved. "It will do her good, poor thing! She hasn't eat a morsel to-day, only sat tinking. Let her hab. her cry out."

"It's been upon me for a week," murmured Susan, between her sobs. "I've felt it comin' on. I knowed it was some great trouble; but I didn't tink ob dis. I didn't tink Mr. Bennet would eber sell Sam! What was we brought into de world for, I wonder? God wasn't good to put us here!"

"Don't talk so, honey," said Lizzie, putting her arms round her. "Tink what Aunt Phillis said. We mustn't question God. He do eberyting best, ef we can't see."

"You neber had such trouble, Lizzie," said Susan, bending her face down upon her hands. "Ef you had, your heart would break. You don't know what it is."

The child, wakened suddenly by its mother's sobs, had begun to cry. Dinah lifted it from the floor, and gently forced it into its mother's arms.

"Try to bear it better for de sake ob de baby. You ought to tink dis is left to you," she said.

"I wish it hab neber been born," said Susan, taking it in her arms, and gazing at it with a strange look. "How do I know what it will come to? No comfort to me I know."

What could either of them reply? Millicent shrank out of the doorway. The scene passing before her was too painful to look upon longer, and she felt as if intruding upon its sacredness.

CHAPTER XI.

AUGUSTA LEESON had fully decided upon severing her engagement with her cousin on the evening on which she had become an accidental listener to his conversation with his mother; but a very little reflection showed her that the announcement could not be made with propriety while under the shelter of his roof. It was necessary, too, that she should first acquaint her guardian with her intentions, and she began to try to think of some pretext for shortening her visit. She had answered her aunt, in reply to that lady's search for information, that her stay would extend to the middle of November, still rather more than four weeks distant. How

85

was this awkward avowal to be got over?
She would write to Mr. Stuart, her guardian, and solicit her recall home. She
did so that evening, after she had retired
to her chamber, from an apparently agreeable play at chess with Mr. Leeson, and
well aware that he would attribute this
singular step, for which she could offer
no sufficient reasons, to a lovers' quarrel.
She stated that Mr. Frederick Leeson
would be her escort upon her return, and
in all probability spend some short time
with them. The answer came, worded as
she had anticipated. Mr. Stuart gladly gave
consent to his ward's return, and fixed an
early day for her appearance at Tudor
Hall.

Augusta went down with her letter to
her aunt. Mrs. Leeson heard the announcement with extreme surprise. Mr. Stuart
gave no reason for shortening his ward's
visit; he left the suggestion of probabili-
ties to the ready fancy of the young lady.

"Mr. Stuart may be ill," observed Au-

gusta, blushing at the ingenious surmise, to
which the gentleman's own familiar handwriting gave the denial, " or Miss Stuart
may be indisposed. She had a severe attack of fever last summer, and her constitution is naturally delicate. They would
not wish to alarm me."

It was very probable. Mrs. Leeson's
sober face relaxed, and she bustled out to
tell Frederick the unpleasant news.

Augusta was eager to get away. Her
anxiety under the apparent circumstances
was natural. She set out on the following
day, under the escort of her cousin. Her
aunt parted from her with an affectionate
farewell. In her heart she trusted that
their next meeting would take place on
the occasion of her summons to her son's
wedding. The young gentleman quitted
his home under the same agreeable impression, that a few words with Augusta
upon the subject, and an interview with
Mr. Stuart, would lessen very materially
his remaining period of waiting.

They found Mr. Stuart and his sister in
their usual health, to the surprise of Frederick, on reaching Tudor Hall, and very little explanation was given of the cause of
Augusta's sudden summons. But the welcome which greeted the young gentleman
was cordial and hearty, and placing the
whole matter to some whim of Augusta's
guardian, he dismissed his curiosity upon
the subject.

The first opening of the revelation which
was to break upon him came to Frederick
in the changed deportment of his betrothed.
She had always been coy, and little disposed to affect his society, leaving herself
to be sought; but now an additional coldness and reserve was visible toward him.
Lovers' eyes are keen. Frederick soon saw
that some hidden cause of dissatisfaction
existed on the part of his *fiancée*. It
might have seemed an unfavorable moment
for opening the subject nearest his heart;
but he regarded it as otherwise. Such a
course would be likely to bring out an

acknowledgment of the secret pique or resentment for which he sought in vain in his own short-comings to find the occasion.

Augusta listened to him with attention. It was a glowing autumn afternoon, and they were alone on the veranda, where they had loitered coming in from the garden. Frederick spoke with eloquence and warmth; the most careless ear might have distinguished his sincerity. Augusta did not. A cold, hard feeling rankled in her heart: she thought with bitterness of the mortgaged estate which her fortune was to free.

"I am satisfied as the terms of the engagement stand," she said, coldly, drawing away her hand; "the time was fixed with your consent."

"I allowed others to decide for us," remonstrated Frederick. "I gave up to the wishes of your guardian. It was natural that Mr. Stuart should be unwilling to part with you. I was grateful enough at the time to be thought worthy of such a treasure at all."

"A six months will soon glide away," said Augusta, turning aside her face, while her voice kept its cold, modulated tone. "I am quite sure Mr. Stuart has no desire to shorten the period."

"Augusta, what has come between us?" exclaimed Frederick, suddenly possessing himself of her hand. "You are changed toward me. How have I been so unfortunate as to displease you?"

"You have not displeased me, Frederick," said the lady, quietly releasing herself. "To what change can you possibly allude?"

Mr. Leeson reflected for a moment. Certainly he had nothing very tangible to complain of. The change of which he spoke was one rather to be *felt* than of that character which can be expressed in words.

"Mr. Stuart was in his library an hour ago," he said, quitting the last subject. "With your consent I will go in to see him. May I tell him I have your permission to urge my wishes for an earlier day for our marriage ? "

Augusta ·hesitated; the moment had clearly arrived for the stating of her purposes, and the distinct avowal of the change in her feelings which her lover's quick eyes had already penetrated. The time had come ; but, for obvious reasons, she wished the statement to proceed from her guardian.

Miss Stuart's appearance on the veranda at this instant made a welcome interruption; her afternoon siesta ended, she had come out through the drawing-room to join the young couple.

Frederick soon effected his escape, and Augusta heard the library-door close upon him, as he disappeared into the hall.

CHAPTER XII.

ON leaving the veranda, Augusta was summoned by a servant to the library. She obeyed with a nervous tremor at the thought of confronting her cousin; but, to her agreeable surprise, her first glance, on entering the room, showed that he had passed out.

Mr. Stuart was alone, seated at his table, with a half-written letter lying at his elbow, his pen still poised in his stand.

"Frederick has just gone out," he observed, as his ward took a chair opposite, a faint glow of color, the result of various emotions, suffusing her cheeks. "He wishes to shorten the period of his engagement with you. Is he right in supposing that he has your sanction to his request?"

92

"Mr. Stuart," — Augusta's voice wavered a little through the intensity of her interest in replying, — "were you acquainted, when you gave your consent to my marriage with Mr. Leeson, with the fact that his property was largely mortgaged?"

"I was not, my dear!" Mr. Stuart looked extremely surprised. "How did you gain such a piece of information?"

"Quite accidentally, sir," said Augusta, dropping her eyes; "but my information is of a character which leaves no doubt upon the subject."

Mr. Stuart reflected. "I had no suspicions of this," he said, musingly. "Frederick should have shown us more frankness."

"You see," said Augusta, with a little covert bitterness, "his reasons for shortening his engagement."

"I do not know, Augusta," said Mr. Stuart, thoughtfully. "Frederick is an honorable man. I have known his character from his boyhood; he is incapable of a mean or dishonorable action. His pride, a mistaken motive, must have held him silent. He would never be the man to woo a woman solely for the fortune she could bring him."

"Whatever the motive may be," returned Augusta, "he has lost my confidence. His concealment virtually sets our engagement at an end."

"You speak under the influence of resentment, my dear," observed Mr. Stuart. "Wait, and let us consider this matter. But, first, are you sure the information you have obtained is perfectly reliable?"

"I had the affirmation from his own lips, in a private conversation with his mother, to which I was an unintentional listener," said Augusta. "Mrs. Leeson urged upon him this step which he has just taken. The mortgage would fall due in January. By entering into possession of my fortune, he would obtain the means to meet it."

Mr. Stuart sat silent. One of the most painful experiences which can ever come to us in life is to learn the unworthiness of one in whom we have believed and trusted. Viewed from every point, Mr. Leeson had acted wrongly in withholding the fact of his serious involvements from his betrothed.

"Are you aware, Augusta," resumed Mr. Stuart, presently, "that this match with your cousin received your late father's approval; that it was, in reality, the object of his dearest wishes, and that his late will, dated but a few weeks prior to his death, contained a clause to favor this event, if it should ever come within the range of possibility?"

"I was not," said Augusta, in some surprise. "What is the clause to which you allude, Mr. Stuart?"

"It is simply this: in appointing me your guardian, he left the disposal of your hand at my bestowal in a measure. If you were to marry without my consent, you were to forfeit the larger part of your fortune."

"At whose suggestion was this clause added?" asked Augusta, with rising color.

"By no one's suggestion, my dear. Your father took no advice from his friends in the ordering of his will."

"I am to understand that he left a written statement of his desire that I should marry Frederick?"

"By no means! The wish was expressed to me, as his nearest and oldest friend, to whose care he was about to leave his orphan daughter. He knew and liked Frederick, then a fine, manly boy of sixteen, and his evident preference for you, even at that early age, might naturally have suggested the hope which he did entertain of a future attachment. It was natural that your father should wish to see his property descend to one of his own name."

It was Augusta's turn to become silent. Where were the glowing hopes which she had brooded over only an hour ago? The dearest thought of her heart in the dissolution of this engagement, and the opening of new prospects, had been the fortune which she would be able to bring to her lover, lifting him above the straitnesses and cares of his daily profession.

"You will consider this matter, Augusta," observed Mr. Stuart, quite recovered from his first surprise over the discovery, and coming round plainly to the side of his favorite. "Frederick has acted unwisely in his concealment, but evidently from a motive of false pride. I believe his attachment for you to be sincere, above the advantages to be reaped by his marriage. Take my advice, as it would be given were you my own daughter, and pardon his disingenuousness."

Would Mr. Stuart really have given such counsel to a child of his own? Augusta doubted. Yet the old gentleman was sincere in striving to carry out what he firmly believed would still have been the wishes of his old friend.

"I cannot," said the young lady, firmly; "it is impossible for me to fulfil my engagement with Mr. Leeson after this discovery. I have not acted hastily; it is

7

quite three weeks since I gained the information. I have waited day by day for an opportunity to break it to you. My mind is fully made up. Under no circumstances will I marry Frederick!"

Mr. Stuart shook his head. He had seen ladies quite as positive before, who, when the occasion came, wavered in their determinations. A young girl's resentment was natural under such circumstances. She could not be expected to retain faith in her lover, where the faintest shadow of mercenary motives rested upon his suit.

"I shall not allow you to decide the matter at once, Augusta," he said, speaking up. "As your guardian, my advice is entitled to some consideration. I will withdraw my conditional consent to Frederick for the shortening of the engagement, and when April comes round, you will know more fully your state of mind, Until then, I must desire of you a complete silence upon your discovery."

"If he only knew," thought Augusta; but she wisely kept silent.

"I will try to obey you, Mr. Stuart," she said, rising; "at least, while Mr. Leeson remains under your roof, I trust I shall not fail toward him in the courtesies due to a guest."

"Foolish child!" thought the old gentleman, looking after her as she swept out with the haughty step of a queen; "and yet I cannot blame her. What could have drawn Frederick into such an unworthy concealment? He should have been frank with us."

CHAPTER XIII.

~THE DREAM.

MR. LEESON'S visit to Tudor Hall came suddenly to an end. He was summoned home by the alarming illness of his mother. The letter came upon the evening of the day on which the interview we have mentioned with Mr. Stuart took place, and in the confusion and anxiety attending this unwelcome piece of news, the subject was for the time dismissed from his thoughts. His mother's complaint was fever,—a malignant typhus,—which might run a long course, or terminate fatally in a few days. Millicent wrote the short, hurried note of recall, giving him the doctor's opinion that the case was one which presented an alarming appearance.

100

Mr. Leeson hurried away by the morning train, the carriage taking him over to the station at daybreak. He had parted from Augusta on the evening before in the expectation of seeing her in the morning; but the carriage came round from the stable before the young lady made her appearance from her chamber, and a hasty examination of his watch showed him that a moment's delay might cause him to lose the train. He left his adieus then with Miss Stuart, who had kindly presided at his scarcely-tasted breakfast, and with a feeling of disappointment which he would have been unwilling to acknowledge to himself, set out on his lonesome drive in the gray, misty dawn. The thick white fog veiled every object on the road, and drawing back from the window, he leaned against the carriage, forced back into the company of his own thoughts. Only a little day before, — it seemed but yesterday, — he had parted from his mother, leaving her in the fulness of health; now he was hurrying to her death-bed! How blind we all are to the hours which are close upon us,—how mercifully blind!

It was late in the evening when the last train halted at the familiar station, and Frederick got out, quickly distinguishing by the glitter of the stars overhead the carriage drawn up by the platform.

Jim was on his perch, straining his eyes in the dim starlight, as the puffing train put off, for a glimpse of his master.

"How is my mother, Jim?" asked Frederick, stepping up to the carriage.

"Missus be alive, massa; but de doctor he say she be very bad."

She was living! Frederick got in with an order for rapid driving, and in a very few moments found himself at the house. A broad light streamed out as usual from the kitchen; but the rest of the house, under its thick curtains, lay in darkness.

It was a gloomy coming home, passing into the silent hall, no one to welcome him. He hesitated at the staircase in the act of ascending to the door of his mother's chamber.

Dinah came out from the sitting-room to tell him in a low voice that supper was waiting him in the dining-room, and had been waiting his arrival for the last hour.

"I will go up to see my mother first, Dinah," he. said. "Is she conscious? When did the doctor go?"

"He just went, sir. Mistress is more herself to-night; but she has been lying in a kind of stupor most of de day."

Frederick went up. His mother's chamber and the smaller room which she was wont to appropriate as a dressing-room lay to the right. He stepped into the last, the door of which stood ajar. The room beyond, dimly-lighted by a night-lamp, lay in stillness. He hesitated to go on; but his light footfall had caught the ear of the watcher inside, and she stepped out. It was his Cousin Millicent.

"I am so glad you have come, Mr. Frederick," she said, in a whisper. "Your mother is very sick. I took the liberty of writing for you."

"Then my recall home was not by my mother's direction?"

"No; she has not been conscious these two or three days, — not until to-night. I hope I did right in writing you?"

"You did." He took a step forward. "Shall I disturb her by coming in?"

Millicent hesitated. "I believe she has fallen asleep," she said, in a whisper. "The doctor has just gone out. He said she must be kept very quiet. I did not tell her you were expected to-night."

Frederick turned and went out.

"Where is Adèle?" he asked, as he seated himself at the supper-table, where Rose proceeded to wait upon him.

"She be gone off to a neighbor's. Miss Halford sent her away."

To keep her out of any danger of contagion, Millicent had shown a prudent forethought. Frederick approved the step.

The table looked very lonesome with

these vacant places. He soon hurried
through his meal, and went back to the
sitting-room. Here he found a fire had
been kindled in the grate, probably owing
to Dinah's forethought, and the room had
been carefully dusted and set to rights.

He took up a book, which he soon
laid down, unable to fix his thoughts upon its contents. If his mother's illness
was of so dangerous a character, should
not James be sent for? Certainly he
should be written to. He got out pen
and paper, with this recollection, and
penned a note to his brother. He would
wait until the morning for the doctor's appearance to add a postscript, he thought,
as he folded it, and laid it beside an en-
velope. He went back to his arm-chair
by the grate, which presented a mass of
glowing crimson coals. The stillness and
solitude of the room were oppressive; he
tried to turn his thoughts from his mother's sick-chamber and the pale, slender little figure he had seen watching there in

the commencement of the evening. His
own affairs presented a subject serious
enough for his consideration; but his easy,
indolent mind naturally turned from their
contemplation. By and by a light slumber crept over him as his head sank
against the arm of his chair, and the
troubled present was soon forgotten in a
deep and full repose.

The room was filled with the gray day-
dawn when he awoke with a start, and
put his hands to his temples to clear
away the remembrance of a painful dream.
He cast his eyes around the room. Its
deep-green carpet, its chairs, its tables, and
low, French windows,—all were *real;* yet
a moment before he had been standing in
a wide, open plain, amidst the smoke and
confusion of battle, with dying forms around
him, and his own brother at his feet, bleed-
ing from a ghastly wound in his breast.
Some moments passed before he could
shake off the hallucination, the superstitious
awe, which the vivid scene had flung over
his spirits.

"A frightful nightmare!" he murmured aloud, going to the window, and throwing up the sash. "It is not wonderful, this dream," he mused, "after Mr. Stuart's earnest talk. He is wrong, — he is entirely wrong; it never can come to arms! The North will compromise first."

The roll of a gig up the avenue caught his ear, as he still stood by the open window. The white fog veiled every object within a hundred yards; but the rumble of the vehicle was distinct over the frozen ground.

The servants were not yet stirring, and he went himself to the door to admit the visitor. It proved to be the doctor as he had anticipated. Millicent, who had caught the same sounds in the hush of the sick woman's chamber, stole down the staircase before the physician had quite crossed the threshold. She looked surprised to see Frederick up, and in the dress of the past night, which showed he had not sought his bed.

Mrs. Leeson had rested some, she said in answer to the inquiries put to her, and was now awake and quite rational.

"A favorable symptom," commented the doctor, preparing to go up, and Frederick turned back, to reconsider the necessity of despatching his letter to his brother.

CHAPTER XIV.

SALE OF PART OF THE SLAVES.

MRS. LEESON did not die. It was a hard struggle between life and death; but her naturally good constitution triumphed, and, by the middle of December, she was able to make her first appearance in the family sitting-room. Her long and dangerous sickness had wrought one important change in her character; it had aroused in the depths of her narrow heart a human interest in her orphan niece. The young girl had devoted herself to her in her sickness, had shared the labors of the hired nurse, whom Frederick had procured immediately after his arrival, and had shown a degree of thought in the commencement, and a fearlessness of the contagion, little to be expected in one so young.

"Millicent has done well," said Mrs. Leeson to her son, in one of these softened days of convalescence. "I shall never forget the obligations I owe her."

Frederick did not reply; the book he had been reading lay open in his hand; but the absent light in his clear gray eyes showed that his thoughts were far away from the page before him. His mother looked up, attracted by his preoccupation.

"You have not told me, Frederick," she said, suddenly, "of your success with Augusta; we talked the matter over before you went to Virginia."

"Augusta declines to shorten the term of our engagement," said Mr. Leeson, in a cold tone; "such is Mr. Stuart's announcement. I have had no letter from my cousin herself since my return."

An uneasy expression came upon his mother's face.

"Her silence is singular," she said. "To

what do you attribute it? Have you had
a lovers' quarrel, Frederick?"

"No, madam; I am as much at a loss
for the cause of her singular conduct as
yourself. I have written her twice under
the impression my first letter had miscar-
ried."

Mrs. Leeson looked really troubled. "It
is quite six weeks since you left Tudor
Hall," she observed.

"Quite that length of time, I believe."

"Why not write to Mr. Stuart for an
explanation?"

Frederick colored slightly. "I have
thought of the propriety of doing so;
but it is merely possible that accident
may have led to this delay. I will give
her a farther opportunity for replying."

"There is this matter of the mortgage,"
resumed his mother; "it will soon fall due.
Have you settled in what way to dispose
of it?"

"I have seen Bennet, and, contrary to
my expectations, he quite declines to submit to any delay in the payment."

"As I feared," observed his mother, with a sigh. "By what means can you raise the necessary sum?"

"A part I can procure as a loan," replied Frederick. "Mr. Leavitt has promised to accommodate me; but the whole amount is large." He put his hand to his temples. Some uneasy suggestion plainly pressed upon him.

"I see but one way," observed his mother, speaking up with her straightforward, business tact,—"some of our people must be sold."

"I have thought of the necessity," said Frederick; "but I cannot easily make up my mind to it. It is contrary to my principles."

"There is no help for it," said Mrs. Leeson. "Susan must go,—and who else can be best spared?"

"I do not know," said Frederick; "Joe and Harry, I suppose."

"They will each bring a good price in the market," observed Mrs. Leeson. "How large a sum will Leavitt loan you?"

"The whole amount of the mortgage, you may remember, is seven thousand, not a large sum to any one with means to cover it; but a very large amount to any one in my position. Leavitt will loan me four thousand six hundred. The remainder I have no way of raising."

"Except on the negroes," added Mrs. Leeson.

"Yes," said her son, slowly.

"Johnston is over to the tavern to-night," observed his mother. "I heard Miss Bennet say so an hour ago; she came in to see me. He has been there two or three days. Would it not be as well to see him at once? He may start to-morrow."

"Yes," said Frederick, laying down his book. His mind was quite made up. Necessity pressed him to action. "I will send Jim over for him." He went to the door and rang the bell. Rose answered it. "Send Jim here," he said. The girl went out. "I cannot do any better," said Frederick, coming back to his chair. "I always said that I would never part with any of my slaves; but the emergencies of the case leave no choice."

Johnston, the trader, made his appearance in rather more than an hour after the message reached him from Mr. Leeson. Frederick was still in the sitting-room. His mother had gone back to her chamber. He motioned his visitor to a chair, without the ceremony of rising, and took a little delay before he proceeded to open the business.

"You want to make a trade, sir, I suppose?" observed Johnston, leaning back in his chair. "Got some likely hands to dispose of?"

"I have two boys and a girl," observed Frederick, conquering his repugnance to the last question, "which I may sell upon fair terms."

"What's their age and condition, sir?"

"The eldest, Joe, is about eight-and-twenty,—a good field hand, but mostly used in my employ as a stable-boy; Harry is twenty-four, a likely field hand; both are strong, muscular fellows. The woman is my mother's laundress, a very capable girl."

"Black or mulatto,—the woman?"

"A light mulatto. She might easily pass as white."

"Would do for a fancy girl, I suppose?"

"Quite likely." Mr. Leeson made the answer in a business-like way.

"I never buy an article without seeing it," observed the trader. "Suppose you bring them forward, Mr. Leeson, and then we will see how nearly we can agree upon the prices. I have rather a large coffle on my hands at present. Niggers are cheap just now; that prospect of trouble with the North puts 'em down."

Mr. Leeson wholly disbelieved this last assertion; but he proceeded to ring the bell, and told Rose to send Susan in with a bottle of brandy and a couple of glasses. Rose disappeared, sending an uneasy glance at the trader.

Susan shortly made her appearance,—a tall, handsome woman, in a neat dress and collar, whose plainness set off her glossy black hair and pale, creamy complexion to advantage.

"A handsome wench," observed Johnston, drawing up his chair to the table to partake of the refreshment, by an invitation from his host, "but sullen-looking. I'll give you a cool eight hundred for her alone; that's as much as she's worth."

"I shall not part with her for that," said Frederick, shaking his head; "she is worth ten hundred at the smallest reckoning; she has a little child, too, rather more than a year old."

"A child is of no account at that age," observed the trader,—"only a trouble, taking up a woman's time to look after. Come, Mr. Leeson, I'll give you eight hundred and fifty, and call that a fair offer."

"I shall not part with Susan for less than ten hundred," said Frederick, decidedly; "only the most pressing neces-

sity would induce me to part with any
of my slaves."

Johnston demurred a little, but finally
yielded.

"The girl will bring a cool twelve hundred in Orleans," he considered.

The prices of Harry and Joe were ad-
justed with less difficulty, Mr. Johnston being first favored with a view of them, and
the trader prepared to take his leave.
The bargain was closed, and he was to
come over in the morning to make the
settlement, and take possession of his pur-
chases.

"It will be hard to break the news to
Susan," thought Mr. Leeson, as he turned
away from the door, after showing out his
guest. "I will wait until the morning; as
well put it off to the last moment."

CHAPTER XV

FREDERICK'S impression of the secrecy attending his visitor's errand happened to be quite unfounded. The unusual appearance of a trader at Wheatley Place was an event of itself sufficient to excite the lively apprehensions of the servants. Rose flew down to the kitchen, her dusky face blanched to a dull gray, and her eyes dilated to their utmost width with her master's message to Susan. To disobey it the poor girl well knew would prove fruitless; and, with a trembling heart, she gathered up the tray bearing the bottle of liquor and glasses, and took her way up to the sitting-room. The scrutinizing look which the trader threw upon her as she

118

faced him in turning to go out did not escape her attention, and with faculties quickened by her alarm, she stole out by a side-door to the veranda on leaving the room, instead of proceeding back to the kitchen.

It was a gray December twilight, and a drizzling shower of rain, which had been threatening from the full clouds nearly all day, was beginning to patter upon the damp boards. She felt very little of the mist or the cold as she crept up to one of the windows which, luckily for her purpose, was not close shut, and, with her ear laid to the narrow aperture, listened to the conversation going on between her master and his visitor. She heard them discussing the terms of her sale.

A cold perspiration started to her forehead, and the strength seemed for the instant to quit her limbs. It would not do to be seen here. She started up as a movement took place in the room, and glided away noiselessly back to the door

through which she had stolen out. She
dared not trust herself with her white
face and startled eyes to the observation
of her fellow-servants, but crept up over
the back staircase to her little chamber,
where she shut herself in. What should
she do? A little girl of twelve, she had
come to Wheatley Place, bought by its
master at a slave-auction in Virginia. All
her life intervening, up to this full wo-
manhood, had passed here. Who shall say
she had not the ties of habit to endear
the spot? But it was not this parting
which agonized her. She knew the fate
to which she was going out; she had
heard it hinted at by the trader. She
crouched down, wringing her hands, by
the side of her little pallet. What *could*
she do?

"If I run away, I shall be brought
back," she moaned. "I can't leave my
child. O Jesus, have pity on me!"

"I must go down," she thought; "they
will miss me." She got up and looked

out of her narrow window upon the dark-gray sky, over which the clouds were rolling up, with a fast-falling shower coming from the west. "It will be a dark night," she thought, as she stood studying the sky. "This gleam of light will soon shut down. I can't but be taken," she mused, as she went down the stairs. "I'll try it, any way. I'm not afraid to die, if it comes to that." But how was she to get away cumbered with the child? Her poor temples throbbed with fever-heat as she tried to think.

At supper she contrived to slip two or three corn-cakes into her pocket when Rose's attention was turned, and Lizzie had got up to go to the stove. Dinah was up with her mistress, and did not come down until their meal was ended. She had to take up her basket of sewing, and to appear as unconcerned as her state of distress would permit. Luckily her silent mood was too common to attract attention, and she heard their uneasy speculations upon the trader's possible errand without betraying her vital interest in the subject.

Eight, nine, ten, came round, and a general movement took place to retire. Susan gathered up her baby, which now lay in a peaceful sleep upon the wooden settle, and took her away up to her chamber.

At eleven Mr. Frederick would be sure to retire, according to his usual custom, and the house would be clear. She got out her shawl and hood, took a warm covering from the bed to wrap her baby from the rain, and going to the head of the long staircase, crouched back in the shadows to which the hall lamp failed to penetrate, and listened.

By and by the sitting-room door unclosed. Mr. Leeson came out, and, with a cloud resting on his usually open face, began to ascend the staircase. . Susan drew farther back in her corner, waited for him to enter his chamber and close the door, and then stole back to her own.

It took but a moment to equip herself in her hood and shawl; another to wrap her babe and lift it, still sleeping, from its pillow, and then, with a step winged to lightness by fear, she glided down the staircase. Her advent was to take place through one of the sitting-room windows, which opened on the veranda. This she had chosen as the nearest and most practicable way. The slipping of a bolt might give the alarm, or even the creaking of a door in the night stillness.

The hall was safely crossed, and Susan had just laid her hand on the door of the sitting-room, when, to her dismay, it opened from the inside, and she found herself confronting Miss Halford.

Millicent with difficulty repressed an exclamation, warned to silence by Susan's sudden gesture of placing her finger imploringly on her lip. She stepped back into the room, followed by the intended fugitive, and closed the door. In one hand she retained her lamp, upon which her grasp had rather tightened than loosened in the surprise of the moment, and in the other a *vinaigrette*, which her aunt had left below, and despatched her for at this late, and as it proved for poor Susan inopportune, hour.

"What does this mean?" asked Millicent, glancing at the hood and shawl and the still sleeping babe, closely folded in its mother's arms.

"Master hab sold me to de trader dat was here to-night, Miss Halford," said Susan, "and I am going to run away."

Millicent put down her lamp on the table, and sat down herself in the nearest chair, in her surprise.

"It must be a mistake, Susan," she said, faintly. "I have heard nothing of it."

"Why should you, Miss Halford? You are from de North, de free country, where de abolitionists lib. Dey wouldn't hab told you of it; dey would tink you would tell us."

"But how do you know? Are you sure?"

"I listened, and heard mas'r and de trader talk. He is coming for me and Harry and Joe in de morning."

"I shall not stop you, Susan," said Millicent, recovering from her surprise a little, and looking up to meet the wild glitter in the woman's eye. "But how can you get away with your child, and in this wild, stormy night?" She shuddered. The rain was beating in a torrent on the hard ground.

"I don't know," said Susan, wearily; "but I'm going, and perhaps de Lord will provide for me."

"You have. friends to help you?" said Millicent, inquiringly. "You needn't fear to trust me, Susan."

"No, Miss Halford, I habn't one. I don't know where I'm going, or how I shall get away."

Millicent looked at her. Was it a secret voice which whispered it to be her duty to give all the help she could to this poor creature in her deadly strait?

"You can never get away on foot," she said; "you will be overtaken and brought back." Her thoughts ran quickly over two or three plans, coming back to their first starting-point. "The train passes at the station above here at eight in the morning; if you could get on board —"

Susan shook her head. "I've no money, Miss Halford, — only a few cents."

Millicent put her hand into her pocket, bringing out her purse. "How fortunate," she murmured, still keeping her voice down to the level of a whisper, "that I should have had this with me! Here is enough to buy your ticket to ——. I wish it were more. I don't know what you will do the rest of the way."

"Thank you a thousand times, Miss Halford," faltered Susan, pressing her lips to her hand. "Only let me get a good start from here, and I shall get safe. The Lord certainly heard me to-night."

"If you can only get to Philadelphia," said Millicent; "but I can't tell you anything about the way." A gust of wind shook one of the windows; both started. "I dare not stay longer," whispered Millicent, starting up. "Aunt Leeson will be impatient, and send for me."

She took up her lamp, and, without trusting herself with another look or word to the trembling woman before her, started to the door.

CHAPTER XVI.

THE FRUITLESS SEARCH.

ON returning to her aunt's chamber, Millicent found Mrs. Leeson impatiently waiting for her appearance with the *vinaigrette*. She had not yet given up the habit, acquired in the first weeks of her aunt's convalescence, of sleeping on a little pallet in her dressing-room to be in readiness to her call, should she require attention during the night.

"You look pale, Millicent," she observed, as she took the smelling-bottle from her hand. "You have not met with a fright?"

"No, ma'am." Millicent tried to steady her voice, and to make a change of position which would conceal her face, under the pretence of stooping to adjust her aunt's pillows.

"Frederick was not up?" persisted Mrs. Leeson.

"No, ma'am; I heard him pass up to his chamber an hour ago."

Mrs. Leeson laid herself back upon her pillows with a languid sigh, and Millicent prepared to go out. The rain-drops were beating heavily against the window; she shuddered as she thought of the poor wayfarer outside. It was quite two miles to the second station. Could she find her way through the wet roads in the impenetrable darkness?

Little sleep visited Millicent's pillow that night. Once or twice she fell into a troubled dream, to wake from it with the oppressive sense of a nightmare weighing upon her; and toward day-dawn she was glad to distinguish a temporary lull in the outside elements, and by and by to discover that the rain had ceased altogether. She lay waiting for some signs of life in the house before venturing to rise, and when she at last did so, the day was far

9

advanced. The storm of the past night was over; a clear blue sky spread overhead, and the sun was coming up royally in the east. Millicent had a difficult task before her. She went down at the breakfast-bell with a fluttering heart. Mr. Leeson had just made his appearance; Adéle came in at the same moment; Mrs. Leeson still breakfasted in her chamber. Susan's flight had not yet been discovered. It was close upon eight; Millicent had stopped to look at her aunt's watch upon the table on coming down. She allowed herself to be helped to one of the hot rolls, and poured out Mr. Leeson's coffee with as steady a hand as she could assume.

"You are looking pale, Millicent," observed Frederick, who seemed unusually preoccupied, his attention drawn to her near the close of the repast. "You confine yourself too closely to my mother. All invalids are inclined to be exacting. You should urge your claims to more recreation."

"I am quite well," said Millicent, her voice dropping. "The wildness of the storm last night has unsettled my nerves."

"The hail pattered heavily against my windows," observed Frederick; "it was severe enough to keep any one waking."

They had not left the table when Mr. Johnston was announced. Frederick rose to go in to see him. He stopped to tell Rose to call Susan. The girl hesitated. Something in her bewildered manner made her master stop.

"I don't know where she is, sir," she said. "She hasn't made her 'pearance in de kitchen for dis whole morning; and Dinah she went up to her room a minute ago, and she wasn't dere."

Mr. Leeson came to a full stop. "Where can she be gone?" he exclaimed. "Search for her at once, and send her into the sitting-room." He kept on his way out.

Millicent sat trembling. It was now past eight; the train had started out. Rose disappeared on her useless errand.

Several moments passed, when Mr. Leeson again made his appearance. Dinah entered at the same instant by the opposite door.

"Nothing can be found of her, sir!" she exclaimed, speaking to her master. "Her bed hasn't been slept in."

The case was plain at last. Susan had run off.

Frederick stifled an oath which sprang to his lips. It was pardonable in the heat of his vexation.

"Has she taken her child?" he asked. "When was she seen last?"

"She went up to her chamber wid us last night, sir, jest de same as usual. We heard nothing afterwards. I's jest asked Rose and Lizzie."

Frederick took a quick step back to the door of the sitting-room. Millicent heard his hurried exclamation to the man inside.

"The girl has run off it seems, — went off last night. I have got to search after her. Will you wait here till I come back?"

"No; I'll join in the hunt, Mr. Leeson. It's lucky I didn't pay down for her last night, I reckon."

"She can't have got far with the child —" said Frederick; the closing of the door shut out the remainder of the sentence.

"Mistress wants to see you, Miss Halford," said Dinah, putting her head in from the hall; and Millicent got up from the table to go up to her aunt's chamber. She obeyed the summons with no little anxiety. Did Mrs. Leeson suspect her of aiding in poor Susan's flight? If such a suspicion should enter into the lady's mind, her agitation of the past night would tell seriously against her. She found her aunt wrapped up in her dressing-gown in her easy-chair by the fire, a table littered with the remains of her breakfast at her side.

"What is all this confusion about, Millicent?" she asked, querulously, without turning round at her niece's entrance. "I

can make little of it out of Dinah. What
is the trouble?"

The girl had evidently been afraid to
impart to her mistress in her still weak
and excitable state the fact of her fellow-
servant's flight.

"I believe Susan has run off," said Millicent, thinking it best to tell the worst.

"Run off!" Mrs. Leeson's face expressed a mute consternation. "Nonsense!
She wouldn't leave her baby; she's somewhere round. Has Johnston come?"

"Yes, ma'am; he is below, — just starting off with Mr. Frederick in search of
her."

It was true. Mrs. Leeson folded her
hands together with a deep-drawn breath.
"She can't have got far!" she exclaimed.
"I heard the hail beat against the shut-
ters long after midnight."

Millicent bustled about, making a show
of putting the chamber to rights, and
keeping her face carefully out of the
range of her aunt's observation.

"How could she have found out that Frederick meant to sell her?" queried Mrs. Leeson. "I can't imagine. Some carelessness on his part. It is just like him."

Millicent turned to go out, relieved that her part in the poor slave's escape was still unsuspected. She went up to her chamber, and closed the door upon herself, to wait, to hope, and pray.

CHAPTER XVII.

THE HOLIDAYS.

FREDERICK returned unsuccessful from his search, to his great disappointment and vexation. The wild storm of the night, which he had trusted would impede the progress of the fugitive, had, in reality, mercifully sheltered her flight. He could discover no trace of the course she had taken, and all inquiries had proved worse than useless. As to the railroad-station, by the interposition of a merciful Providence, that route never entered his thoughts. It might have been comparatively easy for her to have effected her escape in that manner under the disguise of a poor white woman; but he knew her to be without means, and never

136

dreamed that any one of his household had dared to commit the capital offence of offering sympathy and aid to her flight.

What could be done? Frederick could only dash off a notice to a county paper, containing a description of the girl, and offering a reward for her capture, and then consider the necessity of making good her place with the trader. As to the last consideration, the money her sale would have brought he needed, and must have. The mortgage could not go uncancelled. Since Mr. Bennet declined to wait his time, another of his field hands must be parted with. He made the election unwillingly, under the hard pressure of necessity; but, as good fortune ordered, it was now winter, and his place could be refilled out of the portion which would come to him with his bride's hand in the spring. It was not in his easy nature to doubt the certainty of his marriage, though his cousin's singular conduct gave him no little vexation and displeasure.

She had chosen to take pique on some silly trifle, — it was a woman's way; but of the depth of her attachment to himself he entertained no real doubt. His mother did, with better means of knowledge, and the anxiety of mind very much retarded her recovery.

December was waning, and still no reply to Frederick's letter from his betrothed. He finally dashed off a note to Mr. Stuart, briefly demanding the cause of Augusta's singular conduct. A speedy reply arrived, but directed to his mother, and emanating from Miss Stuart. It offered a long-pending visit to Mrs. Leeson from the lady, — nothing less than the spending of the Christmas holidays at Wheatley Place, and added that she would probably be accompanied on this occasion by her brother's ward. It need not be added that Mrs. Leeson made haste to give a most cordial answer, and, indeed, at first the letter seemed to act as an elixir to revive her from the languid state into which she had settled since the fever.

An after-thought came to detract somewhat from the pleasure of receiving the
expected visitors. James would be at
home during a part of the holidays, and
no doubt this fact had entered into the
calculations of the younger lady.

It was very unfortunate. Mrs. Leeson
pondered over the matter until her head
seemed turning with the quickened pulsations of her brain. The marriage *must*
take place. Frederick would be ruined
without it.

Miss Stuart and Augusta made their appearance precisely a week from the re-
ceipt of Mrs. Leeson's letter, and three
days later Mr. James Leeson arrived from
Bowling Green at the commencement of
the Christmas-week, to meet with an agreeable and quite unexpected surprise, under
his mother's roof.

The Christmas-week of 1860! Who of us
dreamed, as we looked out upon its snow-
white fields and gray skies, that the an-
niversary of its return would witness our

fair land, from North to South, rent in the seething convulsions of civil war? We at the North, as the low murmurs of the rising storm reached us, said, "The South will never secede; she dare not; for her uprising would put arms in the hands of her millions of slaves. These idle words will die away." But we forgot that, enthroned above us, was a living God, who in the old days sealed the eyes of the Egyptians, and to whom the cry of the oppressed never ascends in vain.

South Carolina had already passed her ordinance of secession, which act took place on the 20th of December, without waiting for the inauguration of the incoming government; and this news Mr. Stuart brought to the Kentucky household to which he came down to spend the Christmas-week with his already present family.

A hush fell upon the little group in the sitting-room, following the announcement. No one there saw the armed hosts which were to overrun the peaceful valleys; the blood-

red fields on which tens of thousands were
to lay down their lives in the awful carnage of battle; the grief-wrung homes,
peopled with the pale spectres of want
and famine; or, in the background, the
ecstatic joy of millions of liberated bonds-
men,—to all of which this act, taken in
the blindness of human wisdom, was the
opening; but each in the space of that
instant felt the chill of a ˙ mournful and
individual presentiment.

"The North will not fight," said Frederick Leeson, who was the first to recover himself; "she will yield to the just
claims of the South, and settle the matter
by a compromise. These difficulties will
blow over. South Carolina is hot-headed.
Her movement is premature."

Mr. Stuart shook his head. "It is easy
to talk of compromises," he said; "but
such is not the character of the Northern
mind. The time, too, has passed for mutual concessions. The South has already
borne too much. Look at the petitions in

Congress year after year to take away
our property! Think of the John Brown
raid! What can we expect from an ad-
ministration which numbers such support-
ers among its first friends?"

"But what can be gained by going
out?" asked Frederick. "Such a step, if
carried out, will only inaugurate the hor-
rors of a bloody war."

"The North will hardly fight," said Mr.
Stuart. "The voice of public sentiment
there will be against the war. In such an
event as an unfriendly separation, you will
soon see the South a united unit, and the
North rent and powerless with factions."

"The government is good as it stands,"
observed Mrs. Leeson, moving uneasily to
a new position in the depths of her capa-
cious easy-chair, and dropping the work
which she held idly in her fingers. "The
new President elect could not interfere with
our slaves if he chose to do so. The Constitution would keep our rights."

"Yes," said James, who had not yet

taken part in the conversation; "but there are other considerations. The South will rapidly rise to power and wealth without the North; it has always been an incubus upon her growth with its one-sided tariff."

"If the separation can be accomplished peaceably," observed Frederick; "but I doubt very much if such a step can."

"Should it come to a struggle," observed Mr. Stuart, "the preponderance, in spite of numbers, would be with our section. The North is a nation of tradesmen and mechanics, devoted to menial labors, wholly unused to arms, and lacking in the courage and chivalry which belong to our superior race. The conflict would not prove a protracted one, and the result is easy to anticipate."

Augusta and Millicent had both sat silent, Augusta turning the pages of a book which she held in her hand, her beaming eye and glowing cheek showing alone that her thoughts were with the speakers, and on some branch of the subject which they had accidentally touched; Millicent bending over her sewing, a little paler than usual, and with one or two anxious questions whispering in her heart.

Would God approve an unholy cause, and set upon it the seal of his approval by a host of victories, should the possible conflict come? Was it true that his ear could be deaf to the groans of the slave under the lash, the baying of the blood-hound in pursuit of the terror-stricken fugitive, or that he could look with approval upon the selling and using of his human children as beasts of burden? *If he did not*, the end was clear. The awful day of retribution was dawning; and in his hand, the North, though a nation of tradesmen and mechanics, would come up firmly to her work. That night, by her bed, she prayed fervently that peace might heal the threatening dissensions of the land; but, as she did so, the face of the fugitive she had helped in her flight on that wild night of storm but a little week before, seemed to pass before her out of the darkness, and her face sunk lower in her hands, as she added, "Yet not my will, but thine, be done."

CHAPTER XVIII.

CHRISTMAS-DAY.

THE Christmas-day broke fair and clear, after a night of mist and rain. Morning services were held in the chapel located about a mile from Wheatley Place, and Frederick ordered out his carriage at an intimation from his mother to take thither his guests, or such of them as should desire to attend. Miss Stuart gladly accepted the invitation; Mr. Stuart assented politely; James, whose church-going proclivities were of a secondary order, declined, with little ceremony, his brother's courteous proposal that he should take his place in the vehicle, and the fourth seat was, of course, allotted to Augusta. At the last moment the young lady changed her mind,

146

and announced her intention of staying at home. Remonstrances proved quite in vain. She had a headache, she said, which must be indulged; she should go up to her chamber and lie down. "Millicent can take my place," she added. There was very little time left to dress. Millicent hurried up to her chamber, and, without pausing to acquaint her aunt with the new turn of arrangements, came back to find the carriage in readiness, and the company waiting. If Augusta's object was to open an opportunity for a tête-à-tête with Mr. James Leeson, her point was fully carried. At the expiration of little more than an hour after the carriage had driven down the avenue, she made her appearance in the sitting-room, where that gentleman sat, apparently absorbed in the columns of a fresh paper, but, in reality, closely buried in a train of not very agreeable reflections. He laid down his paper, on his cousin's entrance, with some polite inquiries for her headache.

An awkward pause followed. Mr. Leeson tried to start some indifferent topic, and turned, for assistance, to the paragraph which had taken up his attention at her entrance. It was connected with the conversation of the past evening, in which Augusta had borne her part as an interested listener.

"If these difficulties should culminate in a struggle," observed James, "which I secretly believe they will, I shall not remain a passive spectator, but take my part with my own section. Kentucky will go out of the old Union, and so will most of the Border States."

"Your brother thinks differently," remarked Augusta, repressing a slightly scornful smile. "He believes these difficulties will yet be compromised."

"I cannot," replied James. "The movement is too widely extended. We shall very shortly hear that each of the States of the Southern section has followed the lead of South Carolina. But as to Frederick's views, when the time for decision comes, I have little doubt that he will be found on the side of the North."

Augusta's eyes kindled; her hot Southern blood flushed up into her cheeks. Woman-like, she had little idea of the intricacies of politics, or the various aspects which this close-at-hand struggle was to assume. Little as was the love she had ever had for Frederick, and rapidly as this sentiment had of late given place to contempt, on discovering what she believed to be his mercenary suit to herself, she was not prepared for this prediction.

"You believe this of your own brother, James!" she exclaimed.

"Why should I not?" asked Mr. Leeson. "You heard his remarks last evening. I do not anticipate a bloodless separation of these States from the old Union, as I have just told you. The struggle may be even a severe one in the commencement; but we cannot fail to triumph ultimately. It will call out armed opposition even here, in our noble State of Kentucky. Brother will be set against brother, and friend against friend. Frederick's easy nature will take up the shortest policy; he will not stand alone."

"You are unjust to him," said Augusta, with a glow of feeling.

"You think so?" said James, stooping to pick up his paper, which had slipped from his knee to the floor, with the air of one struck by a sudden recollection. "It is possible that I am. I beg your pardon, Augusta."

"I need no apology," said the lady, coloring, and speaking up in the warmth of the moment. "I have no stake in your brother's truth or falseness to his country; yet I believe him incapable of the baseness of siding with its enemies."

"No stake in the matter." Mr. James pondered over the remark with some interest. He had not been blind to the coolness existing between his brother and his betrothed in the two days which had passed since his arrival.

Augusta sat at the table opposite him, her elbow supported by it, her face leaning upon her hand. Her heart, it must be confessed, beat with quickened pulsations. The moment was favorable for an explanation. Would he seize it?

Mr. James stole a glance at his cousin, struck by the crimsoning of her half-averted face, and the pretty embarrassment of her attitude.

"Augusta," he exclaimed, carried out of himself in the suddenness of the moment, " why do you marry Frederick? You do not care for him. You cannot be happy together."

His cousin made him no reply. Her face was wholly averted from him and half shaded by her hand. He threw down his paper, and came toward her, moved by an impulse he no longer struggled to control.

" Augusta," he said, bending over her, " God only knows how I have struggled to stand by and look in silence upon this sacrifice! I can do so no longer. I *must* speak! My own secret unhappiness I could bear, but not the consciousness of yours."

"You mistake," said Augusta, speaking in a voice scarcely above a whisper, as she relinquished to him her hand; "my engagement to your brother no longer exists; it was broken weeks ago by a discovery which should have been made by me earlier."

"To what do you allude?" asked James, breathlessly, retaining her hand.

"To the involved state of his affairs, which he has kept back from me."

It was not a new discovery to Mr. Leeson; he had long been aware of his brother's embarrassments. Whether this was sufficient ground for annulling an engagement, he was at present too much in love to determine. He contented himself with pressing silent kisses upon the fair hand in his.

"I shall bring you nothing, James," said

Augusta, after a little pause. "Mr. Stuart, by a clause in my father's will, has the power to strip me of my fortune, if I marry contrary to his wishes. He has set his heart upon Frederick, and this concealment makes no difference in his choice."

"I do not want your fortune, Augusta," returned her cousin; "let Mr. Stuart take it. All I ask is yourself. My profession, in time, will open to me all I desire, and all that your ambition as my wife can claim."

But it would necessitate a long waiting. James recalled this with a sudden chill of recollection.

The sound of the carriage-wheels coming up over the frozen ground startled both. James went back to his seat; Augusta wavered between a retreat to her chamber and a dread of encountering the returning party in the hall. She had scarcely a moment for consideration, when the echoes of voices and footsteps reached her.

Frederick came in first, flushed and hand-

some with his drive in the cool air. Unobservant as he was in his easy vanity,
by some accident the tableau before him
on this morning drew his attention, — his
cousin's heightened color and drooping eyes,
his brother's visible embarrassment. A sudden chill came over him, a painful suspicion. He commanded himself to inquire for Augusta's headache, received her
half-spoken replies, and stepped to the window. The door behind him unclosed; Miss
Stuart came in, directly followed by his
mother. He had time to think in the buzz
of conversation which rose between the
ladies. Was he dreaming? Everything
around him seemed frightfully unreal. Augusta, was she false? His brother, his
playmate, his friend, who had known nothing from him in the many years of their
family tie but kindness, — could he be
leagued to deceive him? The dinner-bell
rang in the height of his reflections. He
started to offer his arm to lead out Miss
Stuart; Mr. Stuart followed with Mrs. Lee-

son; he felt, rather than saw, with an angry thrill, that James was on the point of offering a similar courtesy to Augusta; Millicent and Adéle made up the company. If he has wronged me, he shall account for it to me with his life, though he be my brother, was Frederick Leeson's stern determination, as with outwardly smiling lips he took his place at the board.

CHAPTER XIX.

THE INTERVIEW IN THE LIBRARY.

FREDERICK LEESON'S eyes were fully opened. He saw at last the cause of his betrothed's singular conduct toward him; her contemptuous neglect of his letters, and the coldness and constraint which had of late grown up between them. Her fickle heart had made a transfer of itself to his brother, and James had dishonorably laid his plans to win her attachment. Now that this conviction had once entered his mind, a thousand circumstances rose up to corroborate it. He wondered at his blindness, and saw that the deception must have been going on for a long time. He thought it over in a stillness of suppressed passion infinitely more to be dreaded in

· 156

its results than any stormy outbreak. What should be his course? To rest passive under this wrong was not in his nature. To any other than his brother, in the heat of his hot blood, he would have despatched a challenge; as it was, he hesitated. He would see Augusta, and demand of her a full explanation; then he should understand clearly how the matter stood.

The afternoon and evening which followed, to one, at least, of the party, proved interminably long. James and Augusta, wrapped in their new-found happiness, kept in the background of the conversation which flowed more freely than usual; Mrs. Leeson experienced a depression for which she was unable to account; Frederick, outwardly unobservant, secretly watched every look and word which passed between the suspected couple.

The following morning favored him with the opportunity he sought, as, crossing his cousin in the hall, he begged for a few moments' conversation in the little room to

the left, which, fitted up with several cases
of books, had been dignified with the ap-
pellation of the library. Augusta followed
him tremblingly. To refuse his request
was impossible; the *denouement* must come
at some time; but she would gladly have
procrastinated it. Frederick placed a chair
for his cousin, closed the door, and came
back to take his seat opposite her. Augusta glanced at him; his usual color had
quite deserted him; his eyes wore a fixed,
resolute look; hers fell.

"Augusta," began Mr. Leeson, with his
usually subdued tone of voice and manner,
"you have not yet offered me any explanation of your silence since I left Tudor
Hall, in my mother's sickness. Were my
letters received by you?"

"They were," said Augusta, in a voice
scarcely audible.

"Why, then, were they left unanswered?"

Augusta roused herself to answer. A
bright glow shot up into her face. Why
should she shrink and cower before this

unworthy man who had basely deceived
her; sought her hand only to free his en-
cumbered property? Why should she hesitate to speak?

"On my last visit here," she said, in a
low voice, "I made a discovery which, in
my opinion, releases me from my part of
our engagement. You may be aware that,
at the time I gave you my promise, it
was more in compliance with my guardian's wishes than from any election of my
own."

"I was *not* aware of it," said Frederick,
an answering glow rising in a crimson
spot to his cheek. "May I ask the character of the discovery to which you allude?"

Augusta nerved herself to the answer.
"The embarrassment of your affairs, which
you kept back from me at the time of
our engagement."

Frederick bit his lip till the blood welled
up from the crimson wound. How had
these perplexities got to her knowledge?

The tables were suddenly turned between them. A hot glow of mortification dyed his face.

"Ladies are supposed to have little interest in such matters," he said. "A mortgaged homestead is no rare matter in Kentucky. This is a subject for your guardian to weigh, Augusta, rather than yourself."

"I have my own opinion of the matter," said the young lady, speaking with firmness. "In my judgment this discovery sets me free from my part of our engagement. I will not marry any man whose love for me rests under the imputation of interested motives."

"It is easy to find reasons for what we wish," said Frederick, turning his penetrating eyes upon her. "Will you assure me, Augusta, that no one has supplanted me in your affections?"

She could not answer. The blood retreated from her cheeks; a cold perspiration stood upon her forehead.

"Let him beware," said Frederick, in a

suppressed voice, "the man who has stepped between us, whoever he may be." He rose. "I will not hold you to your promise, Augusta. A woman's hand without her heart is of little worth. Shall I leave it to you to acquaint Mr. Stuart with the close of our engagement?"

She bent her head, without trusting her lips to speak. Both rose. Augusta, on leaving the room, passed up to her chamber. Her pulses were throbbing violently; her head ached. The shock of the communication to her cousin had passed; but the consequences remained to be considered. Plainly his suspicions were aroused, and not far from the right track. The greatest caution would be necessary in her future intercourse with her lover. What if an open quarrel should come about between them? She trembled at the idea. It had blanched her cheek, and stopped the quick beating of her heart a moment ago. It would not do for her to remain in her chamber; her absence would excite

11

her aunt's attention. She got up wearily from the chair into which she had thrown herself, and prepared to go down. In stepping from the staircase, she encountered suddenly the object of her thoughts. Mr. James, probably missing her from the company in the sitting-room had stepped out into the hall. It was not a very favorable opportunity for a private conversation; but Augusta seized upon it in the hurry of the moment.

"I have just spoken with Frederick, James," she whispered. "We have parted in anger. It would be terrible if he should discover the whole."

"It must come out sometime," said Mr. James, indifferently.

"But he will never forgive you; it will bring about an open quarrel."

The sitting-room door again opened. Mrs. Leeson came out in time to see her niece's hand released, and to notice the young lady's heightened color as she swept past her into the room she was in the act of leaving.

"James," said Mrs. Leeson, stepping up to her son and speaking in a suppressed voice, "what does this mean? Are you sensible of what must be the consequences of your folly?"

"Augusta is free, madam, to choose for herself," said Mr. James, without any attempt at evasion, or any disposition to put a false face upon the actual state of affairs, which his judgment might have told him would be hopeless. "Frederick has released her from her engagement to him, and she is free to elect for herself."

"Released her!" Mrs. Leeson gasped for breath, and turned white. "How has this come about? You have had . your part in it, James."

The gentleman did not reply; perhaps he had no answer to give.

Another timely interruption came about. Adéle's light step glided down the staircase. Mrs. Leeson broke away from her son to pursue her way up to her chamber, where she threw herself down upon her bed, feeling quite faint with the un-expected shock which had met her. It was long before any one came to her. By and by she heard Millicent stirring in her dressing-room, and called to her to get her *vinaigrette.*

"You are ill, aunt," said her niece, anx-iously, bathing her forehead. "What can I do for you?"

"It is nothing, child, only a faintness. I want to see Frederick. Can you contrive to call him from the sitting-room without disturbing the rest of the company?"

Millicent did not know; but she went down, to oblige her aunt, upon her errand. The whole family were assembled in the sitting-room, Adéle turning over a book; Augusta her head bent over some fine em-broidery, with which she affected to be busied: Mr. James with a paper upon his knee; Miss Stuart penning a note at a side-table; Mr. Stuart and Frederick in conversation. Millicent had to wait quite an hour before an opportunity was of-

fered to her; this took place in the general movement following the arrival of a
visitor from the neighborhood; she turned
to Frederick and said briefly that his
mother desired to see him.   She was in
her chamber, she added, where she had
been seized with a little faintness.

"I wonder what she can want of him,"
thought Millicent, as he stepped away;
"she seemed much disturbed; something
has gone wrong.   It could not be anything relating to herself."   She thought of
poor Susan, and wished, for the hundredth
time, that she could hear tidings of her
safety.

CHAPTER XX

MR. LEESON went up to his mother's chamber, to find her extended upon her bed, evidently suffering severely from a nervous attack. She motioned him to a chair, which he took in silence.

"I have heard such a surprising piece of news this morning," she said, turning her eyes anxiously upon him, "I cannot believe it to be real. Frederick, have you and Augusta quarrelled?"

"No, madam," a bright spot kindled on her son's cheek, "by no means. Augusta has expressed dissatisfaction with our engagement; it is not her purpose to fulfil it, and I have given her back her promise."

166

"Not her purpose to fulfil it!" Mrs. Leeson's thin hands folded anxiously over each other. "What will become of your mortgage, Frederick? You will be ruined!"

Mr. Leeson's color deepened. He leaned back in his chair with a deprecatory movement. "My dear mother, do you suppose I am ·capable of urging on this matter for the sake of obtaining possession of my cousin's fortune? I assure you I have no desire to secure her hand without her heart."

"But what has brought about this sudden change?" Mrs. Leeson's voice faltered a little in the question; her eyes dropped before her son's penetrating glance. It was plain that he suspected his brother's unworthy part. The question had been unwisely put.

"There is little account to be made for a lady's fancies," said Frederick, coldly. "I will not pretend to explain for Augusta."

"She has promised to marry you," said

Mrs. Leeson, more firmly; "the engagement is of long standing; her guardian will not allow her to break her promise."

"Mr. Stuart," said Frederick, dryly, "is acquainted with my unfortunate embarrassments. I am of the opinion that, if the subject were to come up in discussion, this fact would make a decided change in his feelings toward me."

"How could they have come to his knowledge?" Mrs. Leeson's perplexity deepened.

Frederick thought only of one way. The brother who could stoop to rival him would not hesitate to take the dishonorable part of an informer. His deduction was natural, though, as the reader is aware, wholly unjust. He was silent. Mrs. Leeson covered her face with a deep-drawn sigh. The position of affairs was deplorable enough. Frederick was right; Mr. Stuart would not now be likely to favor the fulfilment of his ward's engagement contrary to the lady's wishes. But whence could the information have been derived? She dismissed the fruitless question with an effort.

The dinner-bell rang. Frederick got up to go down; he saw that his mother was too ill to make the effort of appearing at table.

"Shall I send Millicent up to stay with you?" he asked, as he turned to go out.

"No, Frederick," she answered; "I wish to be alone."

"He knows all," she thought, as she leaned her head back upon her pillow. "He suspects James's falseness. What can be done? There will be an open quarrel between them; Frederick's blood is high when once aroused, and dangerous consequences may come about."

If she could only get James back to Bowling Green, then she would have time to think of other matters.

"I must see him alone," she mused; "but how shall I get the opportunity? His own sense of propriety should tell him that he can be no longer a welcome guest under his brother's roof."

Mrs. Leeson might have spared herself a portion of her anxieties, had she been aware that this impression had actually entered her son's mind, and that he had settled on the following morning for his departure. It was hard to part from his new love under such circumstances, — hard to lessen even the short time they were at liberty to spend together; but the fitness of things plainly required this course. Frederick's manner toward him had undergone a marked change, and it was evident that his suspicions had seized upon the part he had taken in breaking his engagement.

Mrs. Leeson was too ill to leave her chamber for the evening, and in the morning, James, who had arranged to start by the early train, on learning that his mother was awake, sent up his adieus by Millicent. A gloomy depression hung over his solitary breakfast. The rest of the household had not made their appearance from their chambers. He wondered if he should catch a glimpse of Augusta on passing out.

Jim was already in waiting with the carriage. The hand of his watch on the table beside him was approaching eight, and he had reason to hurry his departure. He went to the window and looked out. The bare, brown earth, the frozen carriage-path, and a cluster of bare sycamores were all that the prospect presented. He turned to the table and took up his watch. At that instant, Augusta entered by the opposite door. Her face was pale and her eyes heavy. James hurried up to her and took her hand.

"I could not go without seeing you," he said. "You will allow me to write to you?"

She murmured a scarcely audible yes. She could not do without his letters, though they might bring about a discovery with Mr. Stuart at an earlier period than she desired.

"Carriage be waiting, mas'er," said Jim, showing his ebony face at the door.

"You will be late for the train, James," said Miss Stuart, making her appearance from the hall; and with a hurried good-by to his cousin, and a dismal depression upon his spirits, quite the contrary of his usual easy cheerfulness, the young man hurried out. He had been spared a meeting with Frederick; he was thankful for that; but the wrong he had done him in this moment of departure certainly pressed upon his conscience. It was not a principle of fear; he knew of no point on which he could be found vulnerable to Frederick's revenge; but he felt that he had violated the code of honor in which all Kentucky gentlemen are reared. He had not done it deliberately. A moment of temptation had found him unprepared, and all these after-consequences had followed as a matter of course.

"I have gone too far to retract," he pondered, turning his eyes from the bleak prospect that lay along the carriage road. "Augusta's happiness is bound up in this matter as fully as mine,"

CHAPTER XXI.

DEPARTURE OF GUESTS.

DURING the remaining week of her guests' stay, Mrs. Leeson did not leave her chamber. The shock she had received had brought on a severe illness. The doctor was sent for, and prescribed medicines which were powerless to cure a diseased mind. Where was the money to come from which should lift the new mortgage from Wheatley Place? was the constantly-recurring question which haunted the sick woman's pillow. She well knew the character of the security upon which Frederick's new loan must have been advanced. It mattered little how near or how distant was the day of repayment; it must eventually be met.

"What are your plans, Frederick?" she

17°

asked one morning, looking up at her son, who had fallen into a fit of reflection by her pillow. It was his daily custom to make her a short morning visit, which on this occasion had been prolonged by her request.

Frederick started. "To what do you refer, madam, — to what plans?"

"This new mortgage, — when is it to be met?"

The son looked down at his mother. It was easy to read now the secret of her haggard face and wretched nights.

"I have given very little thought to the matter," he answered. "The mortgage falls due in about six months. I presume some way can be found of meeting it."

"But how?"

"A sale of the rest of the negroes, the horses and carriage, if no better." Frederick turned away his face uneasily from her questioning. "Do not let this matter trouble you, mother; it will be arranged well."

"Our guests leave us to-morrow," said his mother; "Miss Stuart told me so last evening."

Frederick's face was still averted; he manifested no interest in the information.

"You have not spoken with Mr. Stuart?" hazarded his mother.

"Upon what subject? Augusta? No; I left the explanations to the lady herself."

Mrs. Leeson sighed. She well knew the hopelessness of looking for any change in that quarter.

Frederick went out, and in about an hour after, Augusta made her appearance. Her visits to her aunt's sick-chamber were narrowed into the smallest limits that propriety would admit; and it may as well be confessed that, but for the question of outward proprieties, they would have been gladly dispensed with upon both sides.

"You are looking better this morning, Aunt Leeson," observed Augusta, taking the chair which Millicent placed for her, without any acknowledgment of her courtesy, and contemplating her aunt's flushed face, to which her conversation with her son had imparted a transient glow.

"I am very little better, Augusta," said Mrs. Leeson, turning away her face. "Miss Stuart tells me that you return home to-morrow."

Such were their arrangements, the young lady replied.

Mrs. Leeson considered the subject of her next remark. Would it answer any purpose? It would, at all events, be freeing her mind of a duty.

"My dear, I am sorry to observe the state of feeling between you and Frederick," she hazarded. "He tells me that you have seriously proposed to him the breaking of your engagement." Augusta moved uneasily in her chair. She was quite unprepared for this attack. "Have you considered the subject?" her aunt went on, —"the length of time you have been betrothed to Frederick, and the injustice, not to say cruelty, of inflicting this mortification and pain upon a deserving and honorable man?"

"I do not love Frederick," said Augusta, speaking up with an effort. "I should be doing him a great injustice in marrying him under such circumstances. There are plenty of ladies who would be eager to appreciate his fine qualities and attractions, which are quite lost upon myself."

"But the right of inflicting this pain and mortification?" persisted Mrs. Leeson.

"Has not Frederick told you," asked Augusta, facing her, "the circumstances under which our engagement has been broken off?"

"Because of his embarrassed affairs," assented Mrs. Leeson, — "a circumstance to which no true woman would cast a moment's thought. There is a stronger reason which influences you, Augusta, — one quite contrary to this." Augusta's head drooped; spite of her efforts, a bright color came up into her cheeks. "An engagement of such long standing as yours,"

12

resumed her aunt, " to every truthful mind, should hold the sacredness of a marriage. No faith, no trust, can be safely placed in a man who would counsel a woman to break such a promise."

"I have taken my own judgment in the matter, aunt," said Augusta, coldly; "no one has influenced me."

Mrs. Leeson drew a weary sigh. It was hopeless to go on talking. Augusta rose, under the pretence of arranging her disordered pillows, and shortly went out.

On the morrow the guests left Wheatley Place, Mr. Stuart still in ignorance of the consummation brought about by this ill-chosen visit. At parting, he gave a cordial invitation to Frederick to make an early visit to Tudor Hall, which was repeated by his sister. Frederick answered courteously, and without trusting himself with a glance at his embarrassed and silent cousin. She might retain her secret as long as she chose, he thought: it was a part of the duplicity of her character. How

could he ever have fancied that he loved
her? Yet such feelings are not subdued
at once. There was still a lingering tenderness toward 'her in the depths of his
wounded heart. It would die its natural
death sometime; but not to-day.

"Missus has got someting on her
mind," said Dinah to Millicent, the latter
having found her way into the old servant's good graces in the long weeks of
Mrs. Leeson's sickness. "She's a-worrying
'bout Mas'er Frederick; Miss Augusta has
broke her word to him."

"How do you know, Dinah?" asked Millicent, in much surprise. She was well acquainted with the fact of the engagement,
which, indeed, was the property of all the
household, being, in Mrs. Leeson's eyes,
before the events of the last week, as
fully settled as anything in fate.

"I heard missus say so," said Dinah,
with a little hesitation. "I came into de
dressing-room for someting while she was
argufying wid Miss Augusta. Miss Augusta

wouldn't hear any reason. It's clear broken off, — a great blow to missus."

"You shouldn't have stopped to listen, Dinah," said Millicent, disapprovingly.

"I didn't, Miss Halford; the words came close to my ears. I didn't know Miss Augusta was in with missus."

"How could she refuse him?" thought Millicent, wonderingly. In her eyes, Mr. Frederick Leeson was the ideal of an attractive and thorough gentleman.

CHAPTER XXII.

THE POLITICAL HORIZON THICKENING.

THE closing month of winter wore away; the long spring days came round. Mrs. Leeson came down from her close chamber in the mild April mornings to sit at the open window over the veranda, to listen to the songs of the birds, and watch the springing grass of the lawn and the opening buds of the garden, in the luxurious quiet of convalescence. Two little months had wrought upon her the outward work of a dozen years: her thick black hair had become heavily silvered, her smooth brow taken the tracery of long lines of care, and her step grown weak and uncertain. She bore no longer the appearance of a woman in the full prime and vigor of life, but of one fast falling toward age.

"It is James's work," she pondered, one morning, taking a long, sorrowful gaze at herself in her mirror. "Where will it stop?" She had received no letters from the younger son since his return to Bowling Green,—a silence altogether unusual, James felt that he had acted unworthily. and could have little doubt upon his mother's state of feeling upon the subject.

May was now at hand. The wheat-fields were sown; the ordinary labors at Wheatley Place performed. Mrs. Leeson pondered anxiously over the question, What hands would gather in the green springing crops? The mortgage would fall due in July; all the negroes, with the exception of the house-servants, must be sold to meet it. Frederick was hopeful of raising another loan; but various circumstances were concurring to defeat him. Among the most prominent of these was the disordered state of the country, created by the steadily-looming trouble with the North. The war had indeed opened; a long array of States

had passed out of the Federal Union, and
Kentucky stood hesitating on the ground
of an assumed neutrality, which all clear-
minded men saw it would be out of her
power to hold. Large companies of her
young men were already forming, eager
to take a part with the neighboring States
in the coming struggle, and Frederick in-
cidentally learned that his brother, quitting
for the time the practice of his peaceful
profession, had accepted a captain's commission in a mounted troop, and would
shortly be on his way south to join the
Confederate armies. His admission to the
bar had taken place in the first of March.
When this intelligence was received, it was
close upon June. Frederick did not think
it necessary to impart his information to
his mother. In her feeble state it would
cause her no little anxiety; and, besides,
James's name was now tacitly withheld between them.

The time was approaching when Frederick must choose his politics, and make his

decision upon which side he would be found in the conflict. His neighbors, with a very few exceptions, had early chosen. Slaveholders, for the most part, it was no matter for wonder that they should side with the South.

"Neutrality cannot be considered for a moment," was the general voice in this southern section of the State. "Those who are not with us are against us." And two men of fair property and respectability were signalled out as objects of mob violence, — a little of which put in action might act as a salutary hint to lukewarm friends of the cause, or to those who, like Frederick Leeson, were suspected of halting between two opinions.

Mr. Bennet was the first of these. A native of one of the New England States by birth, settled for rather more than the space of a dozen years on the soil of Kentucky, it was natural that the subject of his political opinions should be regarded with suspicion; and this feeling was destined, unfortunately, to be soon increased by some careless remarks which dropped from him upon two or three occasions.

The committee of vigilance which had been secretly formed met in council. A night visit to his house was decided upon, and an invitation was conveyed to Mr. Leeson to make one of the party.

It was in his home that the message reached Frederick, as he sat in his sitting-room alone, the low windows open to the scent of the red June roses and clambering honeysuckles outside.

Mr. Findley recapitulated briefly two or three of Mr. Bennet's incendiary sayings, and commented upon the effects which such a course, if unchecked, would be likely to produce.

"It will be hard for his family," observed Frederick, with the air of considering the matter of the arson. "Mrs. Bennet is ill, I hear, and there are two little girls, beside Miss Bennet."

"The family will easily find shelter; no

harm is meant for them," said Findley, indifferently. " Bennet will be likely to be shot down, if he makes resistance to the destruction of his property; but that's of no account."

Frederick was not shocked — at all events, little surprised — at this last announcement. Blood was already beginning to flow in these quarrels.

"I cannot join you to-night," he said, answering aloud, "for a plain reason. My state of neighborhood with Mr. Bennet is not altogether a pleasant one; some hard feelings have grown up between us on matters of business; and if I were to make one of your party, it would be, to appearances, to gratify a personal grudge."

Findley laughed a low, short laugh. "This is your reason for declining, Mr. Leeson?"

"I cannot find a better, sir." Frederick spoke with calm courtesy.

Findley got up to go. "I suppose it is useless to urge you," he said, "as you seem to be decided; but I don't know how this refusal will be received. People say, Mr. Leeson, that you are a little lukewarm in the cause. It's bad for any man to lie under suspicion in these days. I am telling you the fact as a friend."

" I am obliged to you," said Frederick, coldly. He got up to open the door and show out his unwelcome guest.

The twilight, with a breath of wind which swept by, rustling the leaves of the rose-vines at the instant, hid the move-ments of a slight, dusky figure, which glided off the veranda and disappeared through the open side-door into the house.

Rose, full of a troubled curiosity — which had possessed her ever since the evening of poor Susan's sale, and the knowledge of her master's embar-rassments, which had got to her ears by overhearing her mistress' talk — to know the errand of her master's visitor, had found a listening place outside the

window, and gathered the most of the
conversation after the first few sentences.

"Poor Mas'er Bennet!" she exclaimed,
bursting into the kitchen, which happened
to be tenanted by Lizzie. "What does you
tink, Lizzie? Dey be going to burn down
his house to-night, and shoot him like a
dog!"

"You go 'way," said Lizzie, turning an
incredulous eye on her dusky fellow-servant. "You're jest trying to make me
b'lieve some great tings, dat's all."

"It's true, Lizzie, ebery word. I listened and heard mas'er talk. I was
crouched up on de veranda."

"What has happened, Rose?" asked
Millicent, who came in at the moment,
stopping short at sight of the two dis-
mayed faces.

Each hesitated to tell her.

"It's 'bout Mas'er Bennet, Miss Halford,"
said Lizzie, speaking. "Rose, she heard
Mas'er Frederick say they was going — a
gang of 'em white gemmen — to burn

down Mas'er Bennet's house to-night and shoot him."

Millicent turned pale. She had heard of such frightful scenes of violence more than once of late. Only yesterday she had listened, with horror, to the details of a frightful scene not three miles from them, at a pretty, quiet spot which she had passed in a spring drive with Adéle. The cottage, belonging to a Union man, had been burnt down; he had escaped, by what seemed a miraculous accident, with his life; but his wife and three little ones had been turned out homeless upon the roadside, to be cared for by a poor neighbor, who had little but a crust of bread and a cup of water to offer.

"This is dreadful!" she faltered; "so near us. Can't something be done to warn the man?"

She spoke aloud to herself rather than to the two servants. The distance to Valley Farm, Mr. Bennet's seat, was little more than half a mile, a distance easily traversed on the highway, and which could be made by a somewhat more circuitous route through the fields. She knew very well the condition of the family. Mrs. Bennet, a sickly woman, was just getting better of a recent attack of fever. The two little girls were aged respectively eight and ten. Miss Bennet, the elder, who occupied the relation of step-daughter to the present Mrs. Bennet, was an attractive young lady of twenty.

Millicent roused herself to ask the time set for the attack; but she could gain little information from Rose. All she could tell was that the party were then in the act of assembling at the tavern, where Mr. Leeson was invited to join them; but whether he had accepted or declined this invitation the girl was quite unable to determine, her master's closing words having escaped her.

CHAPTER XXIII.

MILLICENT'S LONELY WALK.

IT was in the first fall of the twilight; the stars were coming out dimly overhead. The first half of the night promised to be dark; at precisely two the full moon would make her appearance in the south.

The attack, then, would most likely begin at an hour before midnight. Millicent calculated accurately. At that hour the family would be in their beds, unsuspecting and unsuspicious. Three hours would be an amply sufficient space of time to finish up the work, and to scatter in a secure retreat from the vicinity of the smouldering ruins. She would have ample time to warn them of their danger, and to make her retreat undiscovered. It required courage; but we know that the most timid can nerve themselves to action under the pressure of duty. Supper was over. Her aunt, she well knew, was at this moment expecting her in her chamber, where it was her custom to spend the closing hours of evening, reading aloud, in conversation, or silent, as the invalid's variable mood might dictate.

"Adéle must supply my place to-night," she thought, gliding up the staircase to her chamber. Her thin muslin dress was soon exchanged for one of thicker material; her bonnet and shawl assumed, and coming down, she made her exit unobserved, as she thought, through a side-door, and glided into the apple-orchard under the friendly shadows of the trees.

A heavy dew had already dampened the tall grass; she made her way through it as rapidly as she could, keeping in the shadow of stone walls till she came to a part of the road which must necessarily be

crossed to approach the borders of Valley
Farm. It was fortunate that she halted
here; for in the next moment a man on
horseback rode slowly past, reining in his
horse to a short walk as he went by
with more of the tread of a sentinel than
the haste of an equestrian hieing home-
wards or business-bound. Millicent waited
breathlessly till the echoes of his horse's
hoofs died away around the angle of the
road, and then, rapidly scaling the high
wall which had afforded her an effectual
concealment, crossed the highway, and
clambered into the wheat-field upon the
opposite side. This she must of necessity
cross in the full starlight, and she quickened her steps, getting within the shade
of a friendly sycamore just as she heard
a horse's footfalls returning over the hard
ground. Most likely it was the person
who had passed her the moment before
keeping up a patrol, to prevent information from being carried to the doomed
family. He went slowly past, and she

13

nerved herself to quit her place and creep hurriedly on.

The field was traversed, a boundary of fence crossed, a fragrant-smelling hedge passed, and she found herself at the end of her walk. The air was odorous with the scents of flowers, as she crossed the garden and hurried up to the front entrance. A negro woman came to the door.

"Is Mr. Bennet in?" Millicent asked, hurriedly.

"No, miss; he went out an hour ago."

Millicent felt her heart sink at the answer.

"Mrs. Bennet then, — show me to her."

"My missus is sick, ma'am. She's not able to see company."

Plainly Millicent's dress and appearance did not speak in her favor. "Some poor white woman come to beg," was, no doubt, the servant's conclusion. "It wont be of any use for her to see missus; she don't like such trash."

"Take my name in to Miss Bennet," said Millicent, despairing of gaining admission in her nervous agitation. "Tell her Miss Halford wishes to speak with her for a moment."

The woman went in, and presently returned, bidding Millicent to enter.

The room into which she was shown was a large, handsome parlor, elaborately furnished, and well lighted by a solar lamp, which the servant had just set down upon the slender marble table.

Miss Bennet came in by the opposite door as Millicent entered. She threw a glance of some surprise at her visitor, placed a chair for her, and waited to hear her errand. Millicent sank down into the offered seat, and began nervously to loosen her bonnet strings; she found her respiration suddenly growing difficult. Each moment might be of inestimable value.

"You have walked fast, Miss Halford," observed Miss Bennet, regarding her with wondering attention. "Has anything happened at Wheatley Place? Is Mrs. Leeson worse?"

"Mrs. Leeson is well," said Millicent, absently. "My errand is to you, or to your father, rather. A night attack has been planned upon your house; it is to come on in a few hours, and I have come to tell you."

Miss Bennet's warm color left her cheeks; she trembled, and turned white.

"Papa must be told," she said, starting up. "What shall we do? What will become of us?"

"Is Mr. Bennet at home?" asked Millicent, anxiously. "The woman who let me in said he was out."

"He has come back," said Miss Bennet, disappearing through the door.

Millicent sat in anxious suspense for several moments, when the young lady reappeared, and desired her to follow her. She was shown into a small room which seemed applied to the purposes of a library by the hanging cases of books which ornamented its walls. Mr. Bennet, a gray-headed man, sat in a leather-covered chair before his writing-desk, a half-written sheet at his elbow, his pen lying beside it, apparently dropped from his hand at his daughter's entrance.

"Repeat to my father what you have told me," said Miss Bennet, placing a chair for her visitor, "and how you came by your knowledge."

"Did Mr. Leeson send you?" asked Mr. Bennet, bending a searching look upon the young girl.

Was her errand doubted? Millicent felt quite faint. "No, sir," she said, hurriedly; "one of the servants overheard the talk. The company are now at the tavern forming, and they sent to ask Mr. Leeson to join them."

The girl's pale face, coupled with her agitation, told powerfully for the truth of her words.

Mr. Bennet dropped his face upon his hands with a groan. It was easy to see what was passing in the man's thoughts. How should he get away his family, — his

sick wife and two little girls, not to think
of the labors of years wasted in one wanton hour?

"There can be no time to lose, father,"
said Miss Bennet, speaking with sudden
resolution. "I must go up and break it to
mother."

"I have but two rusty fowling-pieces in
the house," said Mr. Bennet, uncovering
his face, "and no ammunition. If I had
the means, I would arm my negroes, and
give these men a warm reception. What
a fool I was not to expect this! But
what have I done?"

He might well ask himself that question,
and so might many another unfortunate
man.

"Where shall we go?" said his daughter, stopping and facing him suddenly, as
she turned to go out. "It will be death
to mother to be exposed to this damp
night air."

"The road is watched," said Millicent.
"I had difficulty in getting across."

"Then they will soon be here," said Mr. Bennet, rising. "Go up to your mother, Jane, and I will call the servants. We must get together what little we can to be saved; that will be very little."

"They mean to shoot you, sir," said Millicent, "if they find you. You wont have more than time to get off."

Perhaps some such thought had already struck him. He began to unlock his secretary, and to take out his papers and money.

Millicent had done her errand. She wondered if she had best linger to afford some further assistance, or if her safety required her immediate departure. The last thought was suddenly checked by the reappearance of Miss Bennet, leading her mother, whose ghastly face and tottering steps showed her unfitness for the brutal scene about to be inaugurated.

"You must fly, Harry!" she exclaimed, addressing her husband. "It is you they want; they will do us no harm. We shall

get shelter at a neighbor's. Did you say
the road was watched, young lady?"

"Yes, ma'am; but there are fields all
back of here which he can get throug

"Don't stop longer, Mr. Bennet," said
the poor wife, wringing her hands: "they
will do us no harm; it is you they want.
Do go! Every minute seems an age."

What could the poor man do? With the
rapidity of lightning, his thoughts went over
his situation, — the uselessness of attempting any resistance, the spectacle of his invalid wife, roused from her bed to be
turned out into the damp, unwholesome
night air, his two frightened little girls,
whose cries, hushed by their nurse, came
distinctly down the staircase from their distant chamber.

"Mr. Leavitt will not refuse us a night's
shelter," said his daughter, speaking hope-
fully. "It's not very far for us to go.
Don't stop to worry any longer, father;
they will be here."

To hesitate was indeed madness. With

a fervent grasp of his daughter's hand, and
an agonized look at his wife, Mr. Bennet
disappeared in the hall, and in the next
moment Millicent saw his figure gliding
over the lawn at the back of the house
in the uncertain starlight. Her mission was
finished; it was time for her to think of
her return, and she rose to go.

"We cannot find words to thank you,
Miss Halford," said Miss Bennet, thinking
with a shudder of the lonesome walk to
be braved by the young governess. "God
will bless you for preserving my dear father's life!"

"I wish I could do more for you," said
Millicent, faintly, as she returned the pressure of the hand which the warm-hearted
girl had laid upon her arm. If she could
but take them with her to Wheatley Place;
but that shelter she knew to be very far
out of her power to offer.

CHAPTER XXIV

THE CONFLAGRATION.

MILLICENT recrossed the road safely, undisturbed by the apparition of the rider who had alarmed her an hour before; but just as she had got safely over, a buzz of suppressed voices stole to her ear, and she became conscious that footsteps were approaching, and that her best course was to lie down in the rank, wet grass as much as possible in the shadow thrown by the wall. The moon was not yet up; a long four hours intervened between her rising. Millicent was quite safe from discovery; but she could not still the quick beating of her heart which the peculiarity of her situation excited. The group of passers-by proved, as she had anticipated

202

them to be, the party at the tavern, set out at this early hour upon their errand of arson and murder.

It might have been that Frederick Leeson's refusal to join them had been considered a proof of sympathy with Mr. Bennet, and they had been led to hurry proceedings from a fear that warning would be conveyed to him.

Several of the party were in a half-intoxicated state, and Millicent shuddered at the brutal oaths and fiendish maledictions which reached her ears. When they had passed on, and the sound of their footsteps had quite died away, she got up to go on. A few quick steps took her across the fields. She glided, with a sigh of relief, under the friendly shadows of the apple-orchard, and stepped into the garden, whose beds sent up a sweet perfume. Here, to her dismay, in turning a corner of the veranda, she came upon Frederick Leeson.

Both stopped short, — Millicent with a sudden thrill of terror at the discovery, Mr. Leeson in complete astonishment.

With more of self-possession, the young lady might have attempted to pass off her nocturnal excursion as a ramble in the fresh air; but the suddenness of the shock quite took away the power of speech, and she stood still with downcast eyes and quick-coming breath.

"Where have you been, Millicent?" inquired Mr. Leeson, his voice betraying a little surprise, while his eyes took in her wet dress and generally embarrassed attitude, which showed in strong effect under the light shed from the opposite window.

"I have been to walk, sir."

"So I perceive. If not too intrusive, may I inquire how far your walk extended?"

"I must beg to decline answering, unless you insist," replied Millicent.

"Certainly not," said Mr. Leeson, courteously, opening the door at the same moment for her to pass in; but a shadow came over his brow. Was it possible that his visitor's errand could have come to this young lady's ears, and that she had started off on a Quixotic expedition, to warn the threatened family? If she had done so, and her act could be traced, the full storm of vengeance would descend upon his head, and Wheatley Place would be the next dwelling selected to become the theatre of lawless violence. The thought was not new to him. He was well aware that, if he should much longer persist in holding aloof from the turbulent majority of his section, he would be set apart as a doomed man, and his home be most likely given over to destruction and pillage. His refusal of to-night to take part in these cruel proceedings had, no doubt, aroused ill-feeling. It became him to be wary how he stood.

Millicent, glad to escape, hurried up to her chamber, to be stopped on her way by an imperative call from Dinah.

"Mistress has been asking for you this hour, Miss Halford. She says come in."

Millicent wavered, but had no choice but to obey.

"Where have you been, Millicent?" inquired Mrs. Leeson, looking up from her pillow. "Adéle has been searching for you everywhere."

"How wet you are, Miss Halford!" said Adéle, looking at her cousin by the full blaze of the lamp. "Your dress is completely draggled, and even your shawl!"

The last, with her bonnet, lay over her arm. Millicent had had the prudence to divest herself of them before coming in.

"I have been out in the garden," she said, speaking quickly, "and I wandered from there out into the field below."

"It is not safe to be out in these times," said Mrs. Leeson, shaking her head disapprovingly. "Don't venture again. But how came you to loiter so long? You must have known I was expecting you."

Millicent stammered something of the stillness and beauty of the evening, and went out, with her aunt's permission, to change her dress.

Mrs. Leeson asked the time by the watch

when she returned. It was nearly eleven.
A little exclamation escaped Adéle.

"How could you be out so late in the
dews, Millicent?" said her aunt, reprovingly.
"Your conduct is very strange."

"I did not dream it was so late," said
Millicent; and the remark was spoken truth-
fully.

Adéle said good-night to her mother, and
went up to bed. Mrs. Leeson was restless, and desired her niece to sit with her
an hour, and read from a book which she
had begun on the previous evening.

Millicent stilled her nerves to turn back
to the third chapter, and commence in her
usual voice the monotonous narrative so
widely excelled by the scenes which were
opening almost within view of their peaceful windows. She read on for some twenty
minutes, when a vivid flame of light shot
up in the western sky, and presently a
broad illumination flashed over the windows.

"What is that?" said Mrs. Leeson, starting up. "A fire somewhere! It must be
near here. Open the window."

Millicent obeyed. The crackling of the flames was distinctly heard; but outside these there was a still and ominous hush. Every instant the illumination seemed to grow more vivid.

"Where can the fire be?" asked Mrs. Leeson, anxiously. "Call Frederick."

Millicent hesitated. She had not heard Mr. Leeson go up to his room, though she had listened once or twice. It was quite possible that at the last moment he had started to make one of the party. She hoped not; but she feared.

"Millicent!" iterated Mrs. Leeson.

She got up to obey her. "Do you wish to see him, ma'am? I think — I am not sure — but I think he has gone out."

"At this time of evening! Impossible. Call him; I wish him to come in and tell me where the fire seems to be. It is very strange it should be so still. I'm afraid it's the Chantilly house-burning over again."

Millicent stepped out, and knocked lightly at Frederick's door. As she had anticipated, no answer came. She glided down the staircase. At the instant she halted on the last step, the object of her search emerged from the sitting-room. Millicent's heart gave a quick bound of relief.

"Your mother is much alarmed, Mr. Frederick," she said, speaking hastily. "Will you come up to her? She is anxious to know the locality of the fire."

It was a piece of information that Millicent could easily have given her. Mr. Leeson had this impression as he followed his young cousin's footsteps into his mother's chamber.

"Where is the fire, Frederick?" asked Mrs. Leeson, anxiously, removing her eyes from the brilliant illumination which spread over the eastern heavens. "It seems very near."

"It shows up from the direction of Valley Farm," observed Frederick, quietly, placing himself at the window. "I think it must be Mr. Bennet's place."

Mrs. Leeson drew a deep breath. "What

14

is it, Frederick,—an incendiary fire? It can't be set by accident."

"It has that appearance, madam. From the total stillness, there would seem to be no attempts to put it out."

"What will become of them?" said Mrs. Leeson. "Mrs. Bennet has hardly yet got off from her sick-bed. She will take her death to go out in this damp night!"

Frederick did not answer; he seemed to be watching the progress of the fire.

"What has Mr. Bennet done?" asked his mother, her suspicions confirmed by her son's silence. "How has he given offence?"

"He has been too free in his remarks," replied Frederick, still keeping his face turned in the direction of the fire. "His New England birth, and the fact that he is a stranger among us, though settled here some dozen years, has made him an object of suspicion."

"What a terrible state of things!" said Mrs. Leeson, shutting her eyes, as if she would gladly shut out the picture of wretchedness and suffering that the crimson sky brought up. "What demon has entered into these men's hearts?"

Below, on the veranda, Millicent's downward glance detected the servants gathered in various positions, watching the progress of the fire. Dinah and Lizzie had joined them; Jim was distinctly prominent in the foreground, a strange expression stamped upon his dark face, which had parted with its easy, good-natured expression on the morning of his cruel whipping. Did a voice, unheard by the curious group around him, whisper in his ear that this picture upon which his eyes rested, — this midnight work of man's cruelty and wrong, was one of the million of opening scenes whose results were to accomplish the liberation of his down-trodden race?

CHAPTER XXV.

THE FRIENDLY WARNING.

THE conflagration of the burning house spread to the servants' outbuildings and the adjoining barn, and did not die out completely until near daybreak. The birds were beginning their morning carol when Millicent laid her head upon her pillow, and tried to forget the incidents of the past night in a few moments of fevered sleep.

It was a weary-looking face which she took down to the breakfast-table at eight. Adéle was there, fresh in her happy unconsciousness of all that had taken place; for the sweet slumbers of youth had kept her eyes sealed through the hours of wakefulness and watching which had fallen to others.

212

Mr. Leeson seemed absent and preoccupied. This was usual to him of late; he spoke but two or three times during the repast, and when it was ended, he took his hat from the hall table, and sauntered out for a walk. He had not got farther· than the extremity of the garden, when he descried his neighbor, Mr. Leavitt, riding slowly past, and, as he slackened his horse's rein, Frederick hurried his steps down the carriage-walk to join him. On several accounts this meeting was desired upon both sides. Upon Mr. Leavitt's part it could hardly be said to be accidental.

"I was setting out to see you, Mr. Leavitt," observed Frederick, when the brief salutations of the morning were over. "My mortgage, I remember, falls due in little more than a fortnight. I confess that I am sorely pressed for the means to meet it."

"Give yourself no anxiety, Mr. Leeson," said Mr. Leavitt, good-naturedly. "I will give you a farther extension of the mortgage, if you desire it. The security is good. Take your own time in the matter."

Frederick expressed his thanks. The relief was certainly a very great one.

"You saw the fire last night, Mr. Leeson?" observed Leavitt, bending a searching glance upon his friend. "I passed Valley Farm a moment ago; the house and out-buildings are a heap of ruins."

"A bad affair for Mr. Bennet," observed Frederick, speaking in a careless tone. "Do you know anything of the particulars?"

Leavitt nodded. "I was one of the party who stood by and saw the work done," he assented, dropping his voice, "though the open road barred the possibility of a listener. It was not quite of my choice; but I had an invitation, and did not think it prudent to slight it. You took that risk, I understand?"

"I did," said Frederick. "But what was the result of the visit? Was any blood shed?"

"No; the family seemed to have received

warning. The house was entirely deserted; even the negroes were not to be found, and the horses had been taken out from the stable."

Frederick looked thoughtfully down. His suspicions of the nature of his cousin's night walk were receiving confirmation.

Mr. Leavitt leaned over, and placed his hand lightly upon his friend's shoulder. "Mr. Leeson," he said, "I have come past here this morning purposely to warn you. I am sorry to say that your refusal to join in with us last night, coupled with the fact of Bennet's escape, has been put under a bad construction."

"I cannot say that this news takes me by surprise," replied Frederick, "though my part has been entirely free from inter-meddling. So Wheatley Place is to be signalled out next? In a lawless-growing community, there are always plenty of excuses to be found for selecting a new object for rapine and violence."

"You speak with heat, Mr. Leeson," said

Mr. Leavitt, soothingly. "In these times, the only way for a man to save his life and property is to go with the strong party."

"There will come a day of reckoning," said Frederick, in a suppressed voice. "When the first terror of these mob days has blown over, we shall see where Kentucky stands. Her legislature has expressed itself for the old Union against the dictates of her governor. I believe it has expressed the true voice of her people."

"I beg you to be warned, Mr. Leeson," said Leavitt, drawing in his reins. "Whatever is to come by and by, we are under mob rule now. I have done a friend's part in coming to caution you. I can go no farther."

"I thank you, Leavitt," said Mr. Leeson, speaking with warmth. "You have done me a great service. If these gentlemen decide to pay me a night visit of the character they gave poor Bennet, I shall be prepared to receive them."

Mr. Leavitt rode off, and Frederick turned his steps slowly back in the direction from which he had come. Two or three unpleasant considerations pressed upon him, — what were his means of resistance, should his house be attacked, and what would become of his feeble mother ' in the excitements and dangers of such an emergency? For the first, he must take the noon train, and set out for the nearest town to get a supply of ammunition, and commence privately drilling his negroes; for the second, it was not best to disquiet his mother with a confession of the state of affairs, but, if possible, to keep her in ignorance. How this could be done in a house peopled with loquacious servants, was certainly a question of some moment. It was best to make a full confidant of Millicent; her position in the household had grown to be one of no small importance, and her daring conduct of the past night, with her after-management of the affair, had shown her to be possessed of both courage and discretion.

Mr. Leeson proceeded to his library, where a part of his mornings were usually spent, and despatched Rose to call Millicent from the schoolroom. It was an altogether unusual interruption, and Adèle looked up surprised, while Millicent's varying color showed a variety of emotions. She commanded herself to desire Adèle to continue on her lesson, and went down with a very distinct consciousness of something unpleasant awaiting her. Mr. Leeson sat in his leather-covered library-chair, with his head slightly inclined upon his hand, and lines of thought upon his brow; but he rose at her appearance to place a chair for her, and when he spoke his voice had its usual slightly-subdued tone.

"I have sent for you, Millicent, to ask your assistance in a matter which I feel unable to fully arrange for myself."

Millicent looked up, a faint glow breaking over her face, which rendered it for the moment positively beautiful.

Mr. Leeson was struck with this observation at the instant.   He stopped for a moment before he went on.

"An attack," he resumed, "is likely to be threatened upon Wheatley Place, with similar results to those of the scene we watched last night.   I shall make my preparations to meet it.   It is of the utmost importance that the danger should be kept from my mother in her present weak state. Will you undertake to do this?"

"I will," said Millicent, the color retreating from her face.   "But are you sure, Mr. Frederick,—are you quite sure there is danger?"

"I think there is; I am quite sure."

Millicent hesitated; her eagerness conquered her dislike to put a question. "What can have brought it about?   You have taken no part upon either side."

"Precisely this, Millicent,—that I have taken no part upon either side."

"Is there any cause, any particular reason given, for these threats?" she asked, her anxiety getting the better of her timidity.

"My refusal to join in the house-burning of last night, for one," said Mr. Leeson, indifferently; "but my position has been a source of dissatisfaction to the vigilance committee, as they are styled, for some time." He paused, as if there was something more he was about to add.

Millicent gave him an anxious attention.

"I shall arm my negroes," he pursued, "and teach them the use of the musket. I am a tolerable shot myself. A few well-directed shots would put a dozen of these cowardly night-robbers to flight."

Millicent doubted. What were the gliding bullets, though winged with death, among a crowd of half-intoxicated and furious men? She got up to go; Mr. Leeson had finished his communications.

"It is not necessary to tell Adéle," he observed, as she paused with her hand upon the door in the act of going out. "We must save her all needless alarm."

Millicent assented, though her judgment did not quite approve this part. She knew her pupil better, perhaps, than did Frederick, and felt that, with a little preparation, her courage could be relied upon even in this serious emergency.

How often we find ourselves rising superior to the circumstances of our lives, — courage, resolution, judgment, developed, which we never thought ourselves to possess! If any one had told Mr. Frederick Leeson, on the evening on which he received his shy, silent cousin into his charge at the New York depot, that the time would come in less than a year when he would find himself depending upon her co-operation in affairs involving the safety of much that was dearest to him, he would have thrown the assertion from him as a romantic impossibility.

CHAPTER XXVI

MR. LEESON took an immediate opportunity of acquainting his mother with Mr. Leavitt's lenient conduct in the matter of the mortgage, an opportunity which he seized upon in the hour preceding his setting out for the railway station.

Mrs. Leeson listened with emotions of thankfulness and relief, which were a little clouded by the consciousness that the troublesome question was only temporarily put off, and must still be met.

"Negroes bring next to nothing in the present state of troubles," observed Mr. Leeson, "setting aside my unwillingness to part with them, and the very serious inconvenience the step would create. Mr.

222

Leavitt can afford to wait; and by the winter, something may turn up. This state of things cannot go on for long."

"The meadow lot may as well be parted with," said Mrs. Leeson, keeping her thoughts upon her son's embarrassed position. "It is hard to have any of your father's estate go; but I see no other way. We must sacrifice a part to save the remainder."

Frederick shook his head. "It would be nearly impossible to find a purchaser in these times," he remarked, "not to observe that the lot you have marked out is really the only valuable tillage part of the farm."

"The waste fields could be reclaimed under proper management," observed his mother. "You have little tact for farming, Frederick; but your poor father had less before you. You should have been bred to a profession."

What had it done for James? The allusion was unfortunate. Mrs. Leeson remembered it too late. The unpleasant news which her eldest son had kept back from her had reached her in a letter from Miss Stuart, the only person at Tudor Hall who now kept up relation with Wheatley Place. It had not been Mr. Stuart's habit to write, and all continuance of intimacy between Frederick and Augusta had, of course, dropped in the new understanding of things. Miss Stuart had alluded to the step taken by James under the impression that it was fully known to his mother.

"It might have been as well," observed Frederick, breaking the awkward pause; "but we could not foresee how events would turn." He pushed back his chair, and rose. "I am going into town, mother. Have you any commissions?"

Mrs. Leeson did not think of any. "I have had a wretched night," she said, going back to her personal complaints. "What will become of that poor family, Frederick? I hear Mrs. Bennet is likely to have a relapse of fever. They have taken shelter with poor Mrs. Crawford, after applying to one or two places. Nobody dared to take them in."

"It is a hard case," said Frederick, musingly. "Mrs. Crawford is poor; it is next to impossible that Mrs. Bennet can get many of the comforts she needs."

"Dinah said she was very ill," observed Mrs. Leeson; "she saw Mr. Leavitt's boy, Sam, this morning. He went to the cottage on an errand from Mrs. Leavitt. Mrs. Crawford had taken some sewing for her. She thought Mrs. Bennet had taken to be a little light-headed."

"No wonder, with her trouble," said Frederick. "It is a mercy Bennet got off. I hope he will make his escape out of the country. If he should be so rash as to hang round here to look after his family, he will be sure to be taken."

"You think they would kill him?" Mrs. Leeson's face expressed a troubled horror.

"We have heard of one or two such instances not far from here," responded Fred-

15

erick. "Mr. Bennet has made himself very unpopular, and by his free speaking put his life very seriously in danger."

"Where will it all end?" groaned Mrs. Leeson. "What will become of us in such a state of things?"

Frederick went out, ordered his carriage, and was driven over to the station.

The train had not come in. On consulting his watch, he found himself a few moments before the time, and began to pace leisurely to and fro upon the platform. Two other gentlemen were waiting, —persons of his acquaintance; but they gave him a cool good-morning, and seemed disposed to keep out of the range of his conversation.

Presently the train came sweeping up; he took his place on board, and was soon whirling rapidly into town.

Conversation flowed freely among the passengers, all confined to one subject, and setting in one direction. Frederick sat silent, only answering when his opinions were appealed to. A grim smile parted his lips once or twice as he listened. The reign of terror had commenced.

Could he have thrown a glance back into his mother's chamber on his railway ride, he might have seen another link threatened in the chain of his sudden unpopularity.

Mrs. Leeson was discussing with Dinah the propriety of loading a small basket with delicacies suited to the needs of an invalid, and despatching it to Mrs. Bennet, whose deplorable condition excited her sympathies more acutely than it might have done, had she been herself in a less feeble state.

Millicent stood by, warmly seconding the plan in her heart, but not daring to add her mite of approval, from a consciousness of the very dangerous mine to which this little incident might set the spark.

The matter was finally decided, Dinah going out to exercise her skill in the kitchen, after listening to her mistress' full instructions of the manner in which to prepare a dish of blanc-mange, and Millicent timidly proffered her services to start on the proposed errand.

Mrs. Leeson demurred, in some surprise. Dinah could take over the basket as well, and Millicent's services were needed in the schoolroom, where it may as well be said that Adéle still sat conning her interrupted lesson.

"I can, perhaps, bring you fuller information of Mrs. Bennet's state. I shall be allowed to see her," replied Millicent, "and —" she hesitated, "will it be best for Dinah to make her appearance there? If her visit should come out, might it not turn to Mr. Frederick's disadvantage?"

"You may be right," said Mrs. Leeson, giving up hurriedly at the last suggestion. "But how will you contrive to escape the same share of observation? As one of our family, I cannot perceive the difference."

"I shall manage my approach more

guardedly," said Millicent, "and I shall beg Mrs. Crawford to keep my visit a secret. Since she has courage to give them a shelter ·in their need, she can certainly be trusted with so small a matter."

CHAPTER XXVII.

THE HOMELESS FAMILY.

MILLICENT did not set out immediately upon her errand. On second thoughts, she dared not trust herself in the garish brightness of noonday, but judged it best to wait till the twilight should render her face and figure indistinct in its friendly shadows. It was a dangerous experiment, this wandering out at nightfall; but it was not again to be repeated, and she would venture this once, trusting to a keen sight and a superabundance of watchfulness.

She heard the distant whistle of the locomotive on the down train, which was bringing in Mr. Leeson, as she stepped out into the field over which she had returned the past night; for she dared not trust herself to the broad highway. Her walk extended farther than that of the previous night, and the road had to be crossed twice, which was a work of some difficulty.

"I wish I had taken Dinah with me," was her secret thought, as she began to consider the increased darkness which most likely would shroud her return, and her very uncertain knowledge of the localities. "What shall I do, if I should get lost, and have to spend the night in these fields?" Her way lay past Valley Farm, the spot she had visited on the previous night; a heap of black cinders and a yawning pit was all which now showed where the house had stood. The fragrant-smelling hedge was scorched, and stripped of its green leaves, the odorous beds of the garden trampled down into promiscuous heaps. Millicent sighed as she looked at the work of desolation, made more dismal in the uncertain light flickered from the stars, and hurried on. A second time she crossed

the road, which now wound to the back
of Valley Farm, without accident, and began to climb the green slope which
stretched up the hill, under whose base
stood Mrs. Crawford's small one-story cottage. She had to pass not far from the
back of a large house, — Mr. Leavitt's, —
and was obliged to make a detour out of
her direct way to escape the possibility of
coming into notice. The deep baying of
a hound struck her disagreeably as she
accomplished this movement, and she started
into a quick walk, which soon became a
run in her nervous alarm. She was quite
out of breath when the door was reached,
and stopped a moment to recover herself
before essaying to knock.

Mrs. Crawford, a pale, slatternly-dressed
woman, opened the door, and waited to
hear her errand before bidding her to enter. Mrs. Bennet had grown much worse
in a few hours, she said, in answer to
her inquiries, and led her into the small
room, which, to appearances, seemed to an-

swer the purposes of both kitchen and bedroom. A fine, sturdy-looking boy of twelve or fourteen lounged on the straw bed in the corner, and a young girl a year or two older busied herself in placing a chair for the unseasonable visitor, after carefully dusting it with her apron.

Miss Bennet presently made her appearance from the inner room, her pale, haggard face and disordered dress forming a painful contrast to the blooming complexion and elaborate toilet of the past night, as did the dingy room, with its confused and poverty-stricken furniture, to the elegant parlor of Valley Farm.

"You are very kind to come, Miss Halford," she said, taking the basket from Millicent's hand. "Mamma will see you; but I do not think she knows any one; she is growing light-headed."

Millicent got up and followed her into the opposite room, which Mrs. Crawford had kindly given up to her unexpected visitors. Mrs. Bennet was lying in a high fever, which was much increased by the close room and the constant excitement which was preying upon her. The two little girls were huddled close to the bed; one of them had fallen asleep, the other looked up with curiosity at the visitor.

"She needs a doctor," observed Millicent, struck by the sick woman's hot face and restless eyes.

"It is the worry which is killing her," said her daughter; "she needs only cooling medicines, and those I was so fortunate as to take with me. If I could only hear from papa, and know that he has got off safe! but I am afraid that he is lingering around here to obtain a chance to speak with us."

"Why do you think so?" asked Millicent.

"I cannot tell you; only I do think so. If he is here, he will be sure to be caught, and they will hang him without mercy."

Millicent could give her little comfort. Knowing the wretched condition of his family, it was only too likely that Mr. Bennet would be tempted to linger in their vicinity to catch news of them, and to form some plan of communicating with them.

"We have friends at the North," observed Miss Bennet, "if mamma was better, and we could only get away."

It was a hopeless plan at present. Millicent said a few words of her aunt's anxieties for them.

"Mrs. Leeson is kind," said Miss Bennet, with a little hesitation. Perhaps the thought that an invitation might have been extended to her mother to be removed to Wheatley Place crossed her mind.

Millicent rose to go. Her visit had not proved, on the whole, a very satisfactory one; she began to see that it would not be safe to repeat it.

She did her errand to Mrs. Crawford, received her promise of secrecy, and, taking her basket from Miss Bennet's hand, said good-night to her at the door.

The young lady followed her out into the air. "Mrs. Leeson has not heard from her son lately?" she asked.

"From Mr. James? Yes." Millicent paused; there was no need to keep it a secret. "He has left Bowling Green, and taken a commission in the Confederate army."

Miss Bennet's face was turned away. Millicent thought she repressed a sigh.

"What is his address?" she asked.

"I cannot tell you," said Millicent, rather surprised at the question. "Mrs. Leeson's information came, I believe, through a letter from Miss Stuart."

"Then he has not written home? Very likely he understood his mother's disapproval of the step."

Miss Bennet said her good-night, and disappeared indoors.

Millicent climbed the hill, and had got nearly past the house, which she had made a wide detour to avoid in coming, when the deep baying of a hound in the dis-

tance again arrested her attention. She
halted and stood still in the tall grass, at
a loss whether to advance or to begin to
retrace her steps. The last was nearly out
of the question, and if the animal was
chained, as was most likely, he could do
her no injury. Very likely his bark came
from his kennel in some outside building,
and was not excited, as her fears had at
first fancied, by her proximity.

CHAPTER XXVIII.

THE FRIGHT.

REASSURED by this last recollection, Millicent hastened her steps; but she had hardly proceeded twenty yards, when the increasing volume of sound warned her that the animal was coming toward her, and led her to halt again, this time in a pitiable state of irresolution and terror. She would have retraced her steps at a rapid run; but her alarm had the effect of taking from her the power of motion, and beside, the distance to the cottage was much too great for her to hope to pass over it without being overtaken, should the hound actually have scented her presence.

Her only course was to stand still and wait the coming of events. The darkness, relieved only by the light of a few stars, was too intense for her sight to penetrate beyond a few yards. She could only discern the tall grass, nodding with blossoms on each side of her, and a cluster of trees in the foreground, which might be supposed to form part of an orchard but for their distance from any dwelling-house.

Millicent clasped her hands tightly together, and fixed her eyes on the distance, from out of which the deep-voiced baying of the dog proceeded, every moment getting nearer. It was a fearful situation. Her breath began to come in gasps, and she was conscious that great beads of perspiration were standing on her forehead. With more presence of mind, she might have tried to climb a tree which stood at no great distance, and whose low branches would have offered a ready foothold; but the terror of the emergency seemed to take away all her thoughts.

Suddenly she grew conscious of footsteps and voices, and just as the dog emerged from cover almost at her feet, with lolling tongue and wild eyes, a hand was placed heavily upon her shoulder, and a rough voice responded to her irrepressible shriek.

"Down, Joles, down! What business have ye here, gal? Leavitt, this is one of Bennet's niggers, I guess."

Millicent tore herself away from the man's grasp, and made an ineffectual attempt to draw her bonnet closer over her face.

"Come, let's have a look at ye," persisted the first speaker, standing up before her so as to bar her progress, as she took a step to get away. "Who and what are ye? Ye don't seem to be a nigger wench arter all, as I can make out."

"I belong in the neighborhood," said Millicent, speaking with difficulty. "I came here on an errand to the house just back, and took this short cross back to the road."

"A pretty time of night for a woman to be walking alone!" the man leered at her with a short laugh. "What was your errand, miss, that you couldn't do it by daylight?"

"I went to carry some things for a sick woman," said Millicent, bringing her basket round from her arm for the man's inspection. "I could not go earlier." She did not say she dared not from fear of the very discovery that had come upon her.

"That's a likely story," said the man, bursting out with an oath. "I say, Leavitt," speaking to his companion, who still kept in the background, and had not once spoken in the short colloquy, "this don't look nat'ral. The girl's a spy and a go-between to Bennet and his wife, loike as not."

"Oh, no, no!" exclaimed Millicent, clasping her hands. "Indeed, indeed, I am not. I know nothing of Mr. Bennet. I only brought some delicacies to the sick woman who I heard was ill with a fever at the cottage."

"What's your name then? Whar do ye b'long?" asked her interrogator, shortly.

"I should rather not tell you, sir," said Millicent, her senses almost deserting her in her terror.

"That's good," said the man, with a laugh. "Come, Leavitt, let's take her along to the house and see what we can git out of her. There's something under this, depend upon it!"

To have kept silent longer would have been folly.

"I will tell you who I am, sir," said Millicent, hurriedly, "if you will let me go. My name is Millicent Halford; I am a governess in Mr. Leeson's family at Wheatley Place."

"Ah!" The man dropped her arm, which he had seized upon in the act of forcing her along, with a short exclamation. "So you are the Yankee teacher; are you? We don't want any such folks round here."

"You have scared the girl nearly to death, Wadleigh," interposed Leavitt, speaking for the first time. "If you have any questions to ask her, why don't you put them in a more moderate way?"

"Like yours," sneered Wadleigh. "Well, gal, answer me one question, and you may go. Where is old Bennet hid?"

"I don't know, sir,—I don't, upon my life! I have just told you what my errand was to Mrs. Bennet; I have told you the whole truth. Mr. Leeson did not know I came here; he has been in town all day."

"Lying comes as easy as breathing to these Yankees," said Wadleigh, in an undertone, to Leavitt.

"Please let me go, sir," said Millicent, hurriedly; "it's getting late, and I shall be afraid to go on."

"It wont answer any purpose to detain her," said Leavitt, speaking up before Wadleigh could reply. "If there's anything wrong, she don't know it. I'd stake my word upon her face! Let her go."

"Pshaw!" said Wadleigh, half-unwillingly. "You're too sober a man, Leavitt, to be taken in by a pretty face;" but he drew a step back, and Millicent took advantage of the movement to hurry past him without waiting for a more direct permission to pursue her course, or for the risk of a change in her captor's purpose. She moved on as rapidly as the thick grass would allow, quite unconscious now of the heavy dews which clung to her skirts and saturated her thin slippers.

The road was crossed, and she turned again into the fields which lay past the deserted ruins of Valley Farm. A sudden apparition started up in her path, as she lingered here for a second, held by some irrepressible attraction to gaze against her will. It was the figure of a man, crouched down in the shadow of the burnt hedge, against whom her dress might very likely have swept in her rapid passage.

Millicent's nerves were unsteady through the fright she had just undergone; her lips parted with a dismal shriek, which rang out gloomily on the still air.

"Hush!" whispered a voice proceeding from the motionless figure, "you will show them where I am."

It was Mr. Bennet. Millicent sat down on the grass. This meeting had quite deprived her of strength.

"Tell me something of my family," he said, crouching back in the shadow of the hedge. "Is my wife living?"

"You don't know what danger you are in, sir!" said Millicent, speaking between her gasps for breath. "They are out with a hound to-night; they came upon me only a minute ago. It wont do for you to linger here a moment; you will be sure to be taken. It may be my shriek has betrayed you now."

Both started, as a breath of wind swept over the tall grass. Millicent listened, and thought she heard the renewed baying of a hound in the distance.

"You must go, sir," she said, springing up. "It wont do for you to stop here! They will be upon you in a moment!"

The man threw a sullen glance at the ruined spot, where so lately his home had risen, without making a movement to stir.

"You have told me nothing of my family," he iterated. "Is my wife living?"

"She is in good hands," said Millicent,

speaking rapidly. "I have just come from her. All her anxiety is for you. If you are taken, it will kill her."

The deep, distant baying of a hound was certainly audible. Millicent listened again.

Bennet picked himself up from the ground. "I have a knife here," he said, putting his hand in his vest, "and a pistol. I shall not be taken alive. But I am faint for want of food; I have tasted nothing for twenty-four hours."

Millicent paused. She had very little time to think.

"I could contrive to get you something," she said; "but how to get it to you? You must get away from here as fast as possible. Where have you been through the day?"

"In a little wood not half a mile from here."

"They will search it to-night," said Millicent. "Oh, I wish you were miles from here!"

They had moved on while speaking, and were now close to the road.

Bennet stopped. "I am not going your way, Miss Halford. I shall strike up through the field."

Millicent, too, paused. "You will not be able to keep on without food. The men are out for you too. If you could hide, and come to the orchard back of Wheatley Place at two, you would then have two hours before day for the beginning of your journey, and the night promises to be cloudy."

It was a good calculation. The fugitive felt. so as he stopped to consider it.

"I will try to do so," he said, "if I am not too closely watched. I know a place where I can hide on the banks of a creek; the water will take out the scent for the hounds."

CHAPTER XXIX

DISAPPOINTMENT.

MILLICENT crossed the road, and traversed the remaining fields without farther accident. She found Dinah waiting her appearance in the orchard in a state of lively apprehension.

"Missus is 'most out of her head 'bout you," she said, as they proceeded in together. "She couldn't think what could keep you so long."

Millicent did not think it best to acquaint her aunt with her adventures; she merely dwelt upon the distance and the alarm which she had really felt in her lonely excursion.

"I should have sent Dinah with you," said Mrs. Leeson; "but the thought did

248

not come to me until you had passed out
of hearing."

Millicent thought it had proved quite as
well. The negro woman's company would
not have prevented the unfortunate rencon-
tre with Wadleigh and Leavitt, and might
have seriously embarrassed the few words
of counsel she had been able to offer to
the fugitive of whom they were in search.
She sat with her aunt rather more than
an hour, and then, as Mrs. Leeson dropped
into a light sleep, she took the opportunity
of leaving her, and proceeded down-stairs.
It was not far from twelve; Mr. Leeson
had just come in from the direction of the
stable-buildings, and was sitting in a thoughtful attitude at one of the windows opening
on the veranda as she stepped out. He
had been drilling his negroes.

Millicent remembered suddenly a book
she had left upon the table, and found it
an excuse for entering. Her cousin gave
a little start at her appearance, and turned
round from the window.

"You have not retired, Millicent," he observed. "Is my mother worse this evening?"

"No; Mrs. Leeson has dropped into a light sleep. I am too wakeful to get rest, and I shall try to busy myself with a book for an hour or two to come."

Her uneasiness was natural. Frederick could not himself shake off the awe of his unpleasant situation.

"I have had two or three busy hours to-night," he observed, speaking in a tone which effort alone made cheerful. "I cannot say much for my first lessons. These negroes are better adapted to handling the hoe than the musket, not to speak of long use."

What motive had these poor creatures to learn? They were not about to fight for home. To-morrow even might see them torn away, bound in a slave coffle, on their way to the cotton fields of Georgia, under the lash of a brutal driver.

"I have read that they make the best

soldiers in the world," said Millicent, with a hesitating manner.

" The full-blooded African, — yes; but this mongrel race, very little can be expected from them."

Millicent did not venture an answer. Perhaps the remark admitted of none. She took up her book to go out.

"I shall have their quarters removed to the house to-morrow," pursued Mr. Leeson. "This threatened attack may come off at any moment. We shall get no further warning."

Was the danger so close at hand? Millicent drew an uneasy breath as she stepped out. She could not be blind to the very scanty nature of Mr. Leeson's preparation. If blood should first be drawn by his hand, it might only have the effect of deepening the fury of his assailants, and hurry his own doom. If Mr. James were only still at Bowling Green, the active part he had taken on the side of the Confederacy would give him influence to protect his brother. Millicent did not consider that fratricidal contests are always sure to work as wide a separation in families as in neighborhoods. In this instance, too, a private enmity added its bitterness, and it is hard to say in such cases if the hatred be the stronger on the side of the injured or the injurer.

It was past one when Mr. Leeson went up to his chamber. Millicent sat in her aunt's room wearying over her book in the intervals of listening intently for his footsteps. She had very little time left before two, as a glance at the watch on the table told her, and she proceeded at once to grope her way very softly down to the kitchen. The night was dark, though a few stars glimmered in the east, and she had to trust to her knowledge of the rooms, and the position of the furniture, as she went on.

The kitchen was reached without accident, and taking the keys of the closet from her pocket, Millicent felt her way to the pantry. Here she abstracted part of a loaf of bread and a few slices of meat, the remains of the previous day's dinner, and stood for a moment casting about in her thoughts for the means of adding to this frugal meal. A couple of dry rolls lay on a plate in the corner. She remembered having seen them in the morning, and felt very carefully over the array of cut glass goblets to reach them.

Mrs. Leeson's closet rarely presented much variety; her table was always frugal, less from her own choice it might be than from the rigid necessity of economy.

Millicent closed the door, carefully locked it, and after wrapping her luncheon in a paper which she had taken down with her, proceeded to grope her way out. She dared not slip the bolt of the side-door, lest in the stillness of the night it should give an alarm, but crept into the sitting-room, out of whose low windows she could easily emerge on the veranda.

The night was intensely still; the air

was heavy with the fragrance of the roses
which climbed around the pillars. It could
not be far from two. Millicent glided lightly in the direction of the orchard, moving
cautiously, and halting more than once as
she passed under her cousin's windows.

The darkness veiled every object around
her. Several moments passed before she
could distinguish the trees of the orchard,
and the spot once attained, she seated herself to await her expected visitor. It was
a lonesome situation. Her heart pulsated
tremulously, and she wished the hour was
over. How would Mr. Bennet discover her
in the darkness with his possible ignorance
of the locality? She laid her ear to the
ground, and listened intently for footsteps.
Twenty, thirty minutes passed. She began
to despair. Could it be that he was cap-
tured? An icy chill crept over her. The
minutes flew on, and by and by a dim
glimmer of light began to show in the
east. A bird began to chirp in the branches
overhead, soon followed by a chorus of
feathered songsters.

To remain longer would be useless. Millicent bent her head again to the ground, only to catch the low sighing of the wind among the grasses, and rose from her seat. She must hurry back before daybreak, revisit the pantry, and make her way as noiselessly as she could up to her own chamber. She had no disposition to sleep; her anxieties quite took away all thoughts of repose, and she sat herself down by the window to watch the full breaking of the dawn.

The negro quarters were early astir. The men had their meals to cook for the day before going into the field, and, if time permitted, an hour or two to spend upon the plot of garden which Mr. Leeson, in carrying out the old Virginian customs, had appropriated to their especial use.

Millicent went down-stairs with the first sounds of life stirring in the house, and passed out into the air. The men were going to their labors in the field, laden with their hoes. Jim, whose meals were taken at the kitchen table, he being considered to belong to the class of house-servants, had just descended from his bed in the stable-loft, and was stretching himself lazily in the sun. Millicent glanced at the negroes as they stepped on in their coarse but whole attire. They looked cheerful and even happy, and one of them was humming a snatch of a song. Certainly slavery presented few of its worst characteristics at Wheatley Place. Mr. Leeson was an easy master and on the whole a fair-principled man. If a portion of human beings had in his eyes precisely the rights and claims of dumb cattle, it was in a measure owing to the fault of his education, and the frightful power of custom. Millicent turned from looking after them to contemplate Jim, whose attention on his part was drawn toward her. The boy's sullen expression struck her. Dinah had lately hinted at a love affair on the tapis between Rose and Jim. Millicent remembered it.

"You were practising with the musket last night, Jim," she observed, speaking to him cheerfully. "How do you like to be a soldier?"

"I dunno, missus." Jim's eyes rolled up with a curious expression. "I's 'most 'fraid ob de gun."

"You wouldn't be afraid of it, if you were fighting for your life, Jim. Suppose Wheatley Place were burned down, like Mr. Bennet's house that we watched the other night, what would become of us?"

"I dunno, miss."

Jim twirled his straw hat over his hands without an appearance of any special interest in the question.

Millicent looked at him uneasily. Mrs. Leeson had been unfortunate in the occasion she had selected for ordering Jim a whipping. She should have given him the lesson earlier, or it would have been much wiser to have omitted it altogether. Although only a slave, it was plain that Jim's sluggish blood had been fully roused by the degrading punishment of the whip.

CHAPTER XXX.

THE ALARM IN THE HOUSEHOLD.

ON going in, Millicent found that the rumor of the projected attack upon Wheatley Place had already gone its round in the kitchen, exciting the liveliest apprehensions of Lizzie and Rose, and the no less deep, but more suppressed, disquietude of Dinah. On closely questioning Rose, she found that the alarm had its beginning in Mr. Leeson's preliminary steps of the past night, which were supposed to be taken with some immediate object. Millicent set herself at work to quiet the servants' fears by assuring them that this course was only what was necessary to be taken by the master of any household in the dangerous character of the times.

They must carefully keep it from Mrs. Leeson, she added, who, in her weak state, was wholly unfitted to bear the smallest excitement.

It was easy to quiet their fears, — easy to put on an outward cheerfulness; but a fever of unrest possessed her beneath. Adéle's cheerful tones grated upon her ear at the breakfast-table, and Mrs. Leeson's fretful mood, when she went up to her chamber, seemed to make more than the usual demands upon her patience.

Two circumstances had occurred to disturb Mrs. Leeson's delicate nerves, — the first, a letter from her son, which had come in by the post the previous day, but which Frederick receiving just at nightfall had thought proper to withhold from his mother until the morning; the second, a piece of news which she lost little time in communicating to Millicent: Mr. Bennet was supposed to be somewhere lurking in the neighborhood, and a gang of men had scattered through the past night in search of him. They had certainly tracked him across a field, and once the hound they took with them had got upon a scent, but was foiled through some unexplained means. Mrs. Leeson had received her information from her maid, Dinah, who, on her part, had been indebted to Mr. Leavitt's Sam.

"It is horrible!" added Mrs. Leeson, shuddering. "They should be content with destroying the poor man's property, without hunting his life."

They had not taken him then. Millicent found herself relieved of one anxiety; the chase had been too close to allow of the fugitive keeping his appointment if he had fully decided to do so. Ignorant, as Millicent of course was, of the circumstances of the previous mortgage, she did not know of any reason why Mr. Bennet should hesitate to accept a crust of bread from Wheatley Place in his hour of need.

Mrs. Leeson made no allusion to her letter, the postmark upon which drew Millicent's attention, as she glided about, placing the room to rights, and gave Adéle, who had just entered, a direction in an undertone to gather her a handful of roses and honeysuckles to replace the drooping flowers in the vases. It might not be for long these little offices would be in her power; she thought over the fact with an uneasy sigh.

Adéle seemed to have caught the contagion of her depressed spirits, as they passed up together to the schoolroom. The young lady had conceived a strong regard for her governess, and Millicent had begun to find in her a degree of companionship which she could hardly have looked for at first. If she had not given her word to Frederick to preserve silence, she would certainly have taken her into her confidence, sure of her judgment and courage under the circumstances; as it was, she doubted the justice of keeping back the peril which was now so close at hand.

"Frederick was drilling his negroes last night, Miss Halford," said Adéle, pausing, with her book open at the morning lesson. "Do you think we are in any danger of being attacked?"

"I do not know," said Millicent, looking down. "The country seems to be in a frightful state; no one is safe but those who are leagued to this house-burning and pillage. Your brother does well to prepare against the possibility of danger."

"What should we do," pursued Adéle, "if they came here as they went to Mr. Bennet's? It would kill mother to be turned out, as poor Mrs. Bennet was, from a sick-bed into the damp night."

"Your brother would make resistance," said Millicent; "he would not leave his house like Mr. Bennet."

"Then they would kill him. You know they were hunting up Mr. Bennet last night to warn him off; Sam said so."

Millicent hoped their intentions toward Mr. Bennet went no farther; on that point she was doubtful.

"I hope Frederick wont resist," pursued

Adéle, with a strange thoughtfulness quite beyond a child. "I don't believe it would do any good; they would only kill him."

"Then you would be willing to see your house burned down like Mr. Bennet's?"

"I don't know; it seems awful. I wish we could go away. Mamma has friends at Belmont. We might go there; they are cousins of ours."

"I suppose Mr. Leeson thinks it best to remain here to protect his property," said Millicent, directing by a glance her pupil's attention to her book. "If he should go away, it would be put to the torch at once; and your mother, even if able to be removed, would not consent to go without him."

The day passed on slowly to Millicent; a feverish restlessness preyed upon her; she dreaded the approach of the nightfall, and shrank from the inquisitive glance which her imagination once or twice fancied directed toward her by her aunt, during her stay in the invalid's chamber.

It was one of Mrs. Leeson's ill days, which might be accounted for, in part, by the oppressive state of the atmosphere, which had gathered a sultry heat, and partly by some mental cause which did not make its appearance upon the surface.

Frederick spent the most of the day in the library, apparently engaged in writing letters, and went out directly after supper for a stroll in the garden.

If the family at Wheatley Place could have looked into the low bar-room of the neighboring tavern a few hours later, they would have found the burden of suspense lifted to give place to a scarcely less terrible certainty.

A group of some eighteen or twenty men were lounging in chairs around the bar at the weird hour of twelve, the land-lord, who, to appearances, formed one of the party, mixing and dealing out a suc-cession of brimming glasses to the de-mands of his customers. A noisy conver-sation was going on, which seemed to have reached its climax, the uproarious oaths and demonstrations for once giving place before the remonstrances of the more reticent and quiet party. The subject just passed under discussion was the plan of attack upon Wheatley Place, — the attack itself had been settled upon earlier in the evening. Only one voice had opposed it, — that of Mr. Leavitt, faintly, — and with a readiness to yield on the first show of argument. Mr. Leeson's unpopularity had come to a mushroom growth, and in the eyes of these guardians of public matters, fully warranted the taking of some bold step against him.

First, he had always been suspected of lukewarmness in the good cause, a state of feeling which, in the emergencies of the times, could be ill tolerated. Secondly, he had shown clearly his disloyal sympathies in refusing to join in the late night raid upon his neighbor, and in privately conveying him information of the contemplated attack. If these causes were not sufficient

to warrant an indignant state of feeling,
another had been supplied the past night
in the fact that Bennet had been clearly
tracked in the close vicinity of Wheatley
Place, whose master had no doubt afforded
him shelter, and where it was by no means
improbable that he was still secreted.

The more violent members of the party
had urged a repetition of the violence offered at Valley Farm, and the summary
execution of lynch law upon the traitor,
who, surprised by this sudden attack, would
fall an easy prey into their hands. The
first part of the motion had been success-
fully resisted on the grounds of Mr. Leavitt's mortgage, and the well-known loyalty
of the younger Mr. Leeson; but the last,
with some little opposition, was yielded to
the decision of the majority. It remained
now to be decided how the attack upon
the house should be opened, and the whole
affair managed in as quiet a manner as
possible.

To call out Mr. Leeson, shoot him down

on his door-stone, with a few brief moments offered him for preparation, when once in their hands, and to search the house and out-buildings afterward for the hidden fugitive, — a search which would then meet with no opposition from the terrified women and negroes, — presented itself as the shortest course.

It was no new circumstance in the heat of this partisan warfare for neighbors to vote the death of a neighbor with whom they had spent a lifetime on terms of mutual good-feeling, or even for brothers to look tamely on and see members of their own households surrendered up to butchery.

In the heart of a slave-holder, used, in his supreme realm, to acts of cruelty and barbarism, little tenderness could be expected; it was rather a ready-waiting field, with the germs of a hundred brutal passions ready to start into life at the hot breath of civil war.

CHAPTER XXXI.

THE ATTACK.

THE night was clear; the heavens overhead were hung with a myriad of glistening stars; the wheat stood in flower along the roadsides; the tall grass, with its withering blossoms, was ripe for the scythe of the mower. Stealthily the party moved on, their footfalls echoing heavily in the stillness on the dusty ground, low words passing between them, — here and there the stifled murmur of an oath, or the bantering of a half-drunken jest. A few moments brought them to the gate which opened on the long carriage avenue leading up to Wheatley Place.

Leavitt passed in last of the company; his ghastly face escaped the notice of his companions in the glimmer of the starlight, and he seized the opportunity of falling a few paces behind them, as they pressed up to the house.

The tall building lay in stillness, the roses and honeysuckles fluttering around the white pillars of the veranda. The midnight band fell back by a preconcerted arrangement into the shadows, only two of the party remaining outside; one stepped up to the door, and gave a loud knock. A little pause followed. Presently Mr. Leeson's head appeared above at the window.

"Who are you?" he demanded.

"Friends," said the visitor below. "You know me, Leeson, — Captain Rodney, — and this is Delford. Come down; we want to speak with you."

"You have chosen a most unsuitable hour for your visit, gentlemen," responded the master of the house, who seemed in no haste to comply. "Will not your business wait till daylight?"

"It is of importance," said his companion, "and we cannot run the hazard of putting it off. Step down, Mr. Leeson; we will not detain you but a few moments."

"I suppose you are armed, gentlemen," observed Mr. Leeson. "In these dangerous times, a man is compelled to be wary of the character of his visitors. I hope you will not consider me inhospitable if I decline to admit you at this unseasonable hour altogether. If you have business with me, it must wait."

"Give us up Bennet, Mr. Leeson," said Captain Rodney, throwing off his first attempt at concealment at this speech, "and we will leave you in peace. We know he is concealed here, and have him we must."

"Mr. Bennet is not on my premises, on the word of a gentleman," said Frederick. "I know nothing of his whereabouts."

"That aint to be believed," said another of the conspirators, stepping out from the shadow of the pillar. "He ran this way last night. We know he's in this house, somewhere, and have him out we will!"

"Submit to a search, Mr. Leeson," said the first speaker, addressing him again. "We'll agree not to do any damage to the furniture, or terrify the women."

"I have given you my word," said Mr. Leeson, firmly; "that is sufficient."

A light step was behind him; a woman's figure had crossed the chamber and glided up to his side.

"For God's sake, Millicent, stand back!" he whispered; "they will see your face in this light. Run down, if you can, and see if they are about to try the windows. Sam and Pete must be awake. I must stay here a moment longer."

A hurried consultation seemed to be going on among the party outside; one or two had emerged into the light, others began to follow. The first plan had failed; it was thought no longer necessary to keep their numbers a secret.

"You had better let us in, Mr. Leeson," said Captain Rodney, directing his voice to him again. "We shall make the search

anyhow, and I can't answer for the consequences if we have to try our own ways
of entrance. I advise you to take the
matter reasonably, as a friend."

A sudden bright flash of light, the report of a pistol, and the whizzing of a
ball, which swept past the captain's mouth
to bury itself in the brain of a companion who stood at his elbow, was the unexpected answer. The wretched man, without a groan or gasp, fell back, precipitating
two or three of his comrades from their
balance, as his corpse sank with a dull,
heavy fall on the greensward.

Another shot followed; the group parted
precipitately, falling back to cover to be
met by a startling volley from the low
windows opening on the veranda, which,
though discharged by unskilful hands, told
with terrible effect from their nearness.
Three forms lay stretched out at their
length on the smooth boards, and their
companions scattered, and took to their
heels in the shadows thrown by the out-
buildings.

"We have routed them," said Frederick, stepping down from the stairs. "Load again, boys, and quick! they will be back. They will try to burn us out," he muttered to himself, in a · whisper. "Thank Heaven, the wind is to the west to-night! If they' fire the out-buildings, the flames will not be blown this way."

Probably this aspect of the case presented itself to the attacking party, for no such attempt was made; but an ominous stillness, broken only by the low groans of the wounded lying outside, prevailed for several moments.

Presently, from his post at one of the windows, Frederick descried three or four figures gliding out from the shadows of the out-buildings over the grass.

"Run up-stairs, Millicent!" he exclaimed, "and see what you can discover from the eastern windows; this part of the house is the weakest, and they will try it again. Boys, bring your guns to a level; take aim! Here they come!"

18

The last words were uttered in a suppressed tone. At the instant a volley of
balls rattled in through the windows, which
parted into fragments of broken glass.
One of the negroes in the act of pulling
the trigger dropped his musket, and fell
forward with a low groan. The rest fired
at the instant, and the attacking party
upon whom the shots, from their nearness,
evidently told, again fell back, and instantly scattered. Frederick found his right
arm hanging helpless by his side, and shifted
his pistol to his left hand.

"I will leave one ball for myself," he
thought, as he clutched it more closely.

The wounded negro lay groaning upon
the floor, his comrades still grouped in
various attitudes beside him. The groans
of the dying outside came with a dismal
distinctness through the now open windows.

Frederick sent one agonized thought to
his mother, another to his helpless young
sister and cousin, and whispering to his

men to reload their guns, waited gloomily the third attack which he had little doubt would follow. He was happily disappointed, however. The night murderers, disgusted with their hot reception, and no doubt be-lieving, on the second repulse, that Mr. Leeson had collected an army of his friends beside him, gave up the attack, and scat-tered in retreat, leaving their dead and wounded stretched upon the dewy grass.

CHAPTER XXXII.

THE MORNING SCENE.

A LONG hour passed, its solemn stillness broken to Millicent on her watch by the sobs and exclamations of the terrified servants, whose voices reached her from the head of the back staircase, where they had crowded together, and to the group below in the sitting-room by the continued groans outside.

"They must have gone," thought Millicent, turning at length from the window, after sending a long, searching glance outside. She ran down the staircase, to come into collision with another figure at the foot, a slight, girlish form, which she at once recognized as Adéle's.

"Oh, Millicent!" she gasped, catching her cousin's hands, "where is Frederick?"

"Go back to your mother, Adéle," said Millicent, trying to speak bravely, while her heart grew frightfully faint. "It will not do to leave her alone."

Frederick, who had heard the short colloquy, stepped to the door.

"I think the worst is over," he said, in a low voice. "They will not come back. It cannot be far from day."

"Oh, you are safe, Fred.!" said Adéle, with a burst of joy.

Millicent's emotion kept her silent.

"You had better go up-stairs again," said Mr. Leeson. "My mother must be in a state of great alarm."

Millicent put her arm around her cousin, and urged her gently up the stairs. Mrs. Leeson was alone in her chamber, lying back on her pillows, with an uneasy respiration. Her hands were clasped tightly together; she seemed to be in the act of prayer.

"Is Frederick safe?" she asked, opening her eyes at Millicent's quick step.

"He is safe, mother!" said Adèle, who had followed close behind her. "He has beaten the men off; they wont come back."

"Is this true?" asked Mrs. Leeson, looking anxiously at Millicent.

"Yes, ma'am; Mr. Frederick thinks they have gone."

"I want to see Frederick. Will you send him up, Millicent?"

Her niece hesitated.

"I want to see him with my own eyes," persisted his mother, — "to see that he is safe."

Millicent went down, groping her way again over the dark staircase.

Frederick was standing near one of the windows as she stepped into the sitting-room. She noticed for the first time that his right arm hung loosely by his side.

"You are wounded!" she exclaimed, terrified.

"Only a scratch. A ball has disabled my arm; that is all. I think we are safe for to-night; they have got enough. Millicent,

can you get some bandages? This poor
fellow, I fear, is badly hurt."

Millicent went to her work-basket, which
she remembered contained two or three
strips of fine cloth precisely adapted to
this purpose. She lingered to see if she
could be of further service, quite forgetting, in her anxiety, her aunt's errand.

The man's wound proved to be in his
shoulder, a very severe one, which Frederick saw, even in the imperfect light, was
quite beyond his handling. He could only
stanch the further flow of blood, and consider the necessity of sending for the nearest doctor as soon as the day-dawn would
permit. It was close at hand; a glimmer-
ing of light had already begun to show in
the east, and the low voices of the birds
to twitter among the bushes of the garden.

Frederick drew aside the heavy bolt that
had barred the passage of his night visitors an hour before, and stepped out on the
veranda. There was nothing now to fear.
The spot was tenanted only by two mo-

tionless forms congealed in blood. The
third had crawled away, and lay with his
face downward in one of the odorous beds
of the garden, his hands clinched above
his head as he lay extended among the
crushed stalks of the flowers.

Frederick stooped over the first corpse,
and gently put back with his hand the
thick, matted hair from the temples. As
he did so, a low exclamation of horror escaped him. The dead face turned up in
the gray dawn, convulsed and ghastly white,
was no other than that of his friend, Mr.
Leavitt.

A low groan burst from the young man
as he lifted himself up. He could not but
see the righteous retribution which had been
so strangely dealt out. He recalled the
dead man's words to him but a little space
before, — "The only way to save a man's
life and property in these times is to go
with the strong party." Had it proved so?
He had acted against his conscience, **and
here was the end.**

The nearness of the attacking to the re-
pelling party had made most of the ill-
directed shots prove fatal. Four corpses
lay on the veranda and in the garden,
each stark and stiff, the last spark of vitality gone out.

Frederick came in to attend to his own
wound, which proved, as he had anticipated, a trifling one, and to despatch one
of the negroes for a doctor for poor Sam,
who lay groaning upon the floor. Millicent gave him his mother's message, and
he went up to her chamber. Adéle was
sitting by her bedside; both were in a
state of painful distress.

"How will this end?" asked his mother,
looking anxiously at him, after receiving
his assurance that his wound, which at
once attracted her attention, was slight, a
mere scratch. "Is any one killed? Have
you drawn blood?"

Frederick hesitated. "We had to beat
them back, mother. Nothing short of blood
would satisfy them. Poor Sam is badly

wounded, I fear. The rest got off without a scratch. If it had been a full moonlight night, we should have fared worse."

"They will come again," said Mrs. Leeson, with a shudder. "We must go from here. Oh, Frederick, what have you done to bring on this attack?"

"I have done nothing, mother," said Mr. Leeson, quietly. "But these last three hours have decided my politics. Henceforth I stand no longer neutral, but espouse with voice and hand the cause of the Union."

"Oh, my son!" — Mrs. Leeson's hands came together with a convulsive clasp, — "do you know what you do? You are arming against James, — brother against brother!"

"I have no brother, madam," said Mr. Leeson. "That relationship was broken months ago."

"I fear so," said his mother, with a groan; "but oh, Frederick, he is still my son!"

"Shall we stay here?" asked Adéle,

whose presence had been forgotten by both. "How shall we get mamma away, and where shall we go to?"

"For the present we shall be compelled to remain here," replied Frederick. "After the repulse and loss they have had, these men will not be in a hurry to return to the attack."

"I don't know," said his mother; "their passions will be quickened by revenge."

"At least we shall have time to think over the matter," said Frederick, rising. "I have some orders to give, and must leave you. Try to be composed, my dear mother; all danger is over. We have great reasons for thankfulness in our fortunate escape."

They had, indeed, reasons enough to draw a prayer from the most irreverent heart.

Millicent was standing in the hall-door, as Frederick went down, in the act of stepping out. He put his hand upon her arm, and drew her gently in.

"These sights outside are not for you,

Millicent," he said, in a tone of grave earnestness. "Those wretched men have paid for their wanton violence with their lives. I am about to send to their families."

"You know them?" asked Millicent, shuddering.

"Two of them; the one farther down in the garden I am unable to recognize."

"Oh, it is horrible!" said Millicent, wringing her hands. "What wretchedness it will bring into their homes!"

An inexplicable expression of pain passed over Mr. Leeson's face. Millicent caught it as she looked up; but she did not dream of its source,—that the friend who had warned him, and through whose well-meant caution he had warded off this night attack, was lying there among those lifeless corpses.

CHAPTER XXXIII.

THE VILLAGE DOCTOR.

THE village doctor speedily obeyed Mr. Leeson's summons, under the impression that he was called upon to attend his late patient, and found, much to his surprise, a wounded negro anxiously watching for his appearance. A few words explained the events of the past night, and the worthy doctor proceeded to call out his best skill for the occasion. The traces of the deadly affray were still visible in the corpses laid out on the lawn, the trampled shrubbery, and the scattered glass and wood-work of the windows of the sitting-room, whose walls and furniture were · marked in two or three places by pistol-shots, as well as in the alarm and excitement which yet pervaded the household.

285

"This will be no safe place for you, Mr. Leeson," said the friendly doctor, on taking his leave, after a kind inquiry for Mrs. Leeson, who was quite unable to see him. "Your life is of very little consequence in these parts after this; you had better take measures to get away."

"And leave my property to be wasted by these villains?"

"No; your family will protect it, as they would be wholly unable to do under the ban of your presence. The house and most of the estate lie under a mortgage to Leavitt, I have been told."

"They did." Mr. Leeson turned away his face.

"It has been paid up then?"

"No; Mr. Leavitt was with the party last night,— *was* with them."

"I understand. This is a horrible affair, Mr. Leeson. But what have you done? I always thought you were a moderate man, and rather on the safe side."

"Moderation goes for nothing in these

times," was the gloomy response. "My last night's experience has brought me over to the side of the Union."

"Every one must choose for himself," remarked the doctor. "My profession allows neutrality; but I must be cautious how I stretch my liberty. I don't know, Mr. Leeson, as it will be prudent for me to pay you a second visit."

"As you like. You think the poor fellow has a chance to recover?"

"A small one. It is an ugly wound, and there will be some infiamation."

"I will send to you for medicines unless you interdict me," said his host, passing with him down the walk. "The poor fellow has been wounded in defending me and my family, and I shall do my best by him."

"Oh, certainly! Send by all means; that can be managed in a way to make no trouble."

The sun was up; the glowing flowers of one little plat in the garden shone with human blood, where they lay thickly trampled under foot.

Frederick turned from the unpleasant sight; the fresh air, the dewy fragrance of the morning, sickened upon his senses with the contrasts around him. He went in to give orders to have the wounded man carried by his comrades to a comfortable chamber, and to desire Millicent to see that his immediate wants were attended to. His own wound was beginning to grow painful; he had declined to have it examined by the surgeon, believing it to be a mere flesh scratch; but, on removing the bandage, he found it to show in the strong light of a more serious character than he had at first supposed; still, it was not likely to prove a serious matter, but one which his own skill could master.

Breakfast this morning was a sober meal; it was gone through as usual. Millicent and Adéle came to their places at the table; but very little was tasted. When Frederick quitted the table, a message was brought him by Dinah, and he went up again to his mother's chamber.

Left to herself, Mrs. Leeson's liveliest apprehensions had returned, and she had sent for her son to urge upon him the necessity of his immediate flight.

"They have no enmity against us," she urged; "it is you they want. As James's mother and sister, no insults would be offered us. The very defencelessness of our position alone would protect us. It is my desire that you leave us, and provide for your safety."

Frederick hesitated. He had listened a few moments before to the same argument. It was his settled purpose to join the Union army, a detachment of which, as he had been for the last few days aware, was now at Lexington, rapidly receiving enlistments. But how to abandon his property, and, most of all, his unprotected family, in the present state of affairs, was a serious question.

"You involve us in your peril by remaining here," persisted his mother. "After what has taken place, your life is in danger at every hour. If you venture a few rods from your own door, you may be shot in broad daylight. The only safety for you lies in immediate flight."

It was not a pleasant picture; but it had the merit of truth. Frederick drew a deep breath, as his mother's thin fingers clasped upon his.

"This anxiety is killing me," she pleaded. "I have suspected your danger for the last few days."

If he could take her with him to a place of safety! Her son thought over the matter anxiously. The recollection of their relatives at Belmont occurred to him as it had done to Adéle; but a second glance at his mother's wan face upon the pillow showed the hopelessness of this plan. She had changed much in the last few days: he understood now that the secret which he had hoped withheld from her had been fully guessed by her anxious fears.

"Once to know you in safety, I shall
be content," she said. "They will not
harm us; we have done nothing to displease them."

It was a hard struggle. On the one
hand, Frederick knew the ineffectual character of the resistance it might be in his
power to offer to a second and better-
sorted attack, which would be sure to be
brought against him, should he remain in
his hostile neighborhood; on the other,
could he be sure that the avowed fact
of his absence would be a sufficient protection for his helpless family?

CHAPTER XXXIV.

MILLICENT'S DISCOVERY.

MR. LEESON'S decision was made upon quitting his mother's chamber. To remain where he was would answer no good purpose, beside involving his family in his danger. He could discern that the present state of affairs was not by any means a permanent one. He had little doubt that an active Union feeling, smothered for the present under the hand of mob rule, pervaded the breasts of many, wanting only a sufficient organization and protection to be called out. This step he was about to take might enable him to furnish the latter at no distant day.

There was little time to be lost. Frederick proceeded to call his servant, and or-

dered him to pack his valise. Then he
turned his steps to the chamber occupied
by the wounded negro, where he had. little doubt he should find Millicent. The
door stood ajar; she was bending over the
couch, with a cup of some cooling bever-
age in her hand.

Frederick's step caught her ear; she
turned toward him, set down the cup, and
came out to meet him.

"He seems very sick," she said, in a
low voice, alluding to her charge. "When
will the doctor come again?"

"I have come to tell you that I am
going away," said Frederick, without answering her question. "I have just given
orders to Joe to pack my valise."

Millicent's face brightened a little of the
shadow which hung over it; she looked
relieved.

"I am glad you are going," she said,
simply.

"I shall set out for Lexington," pursued
Mr. Leeson, "and join the army which is

gathering there. Millicent, I shall be compelled to leave the care of my mother, and the interests of the family, in your hands in my absence."

"I will try to be faithful," said Millicent, her suffused eyes and colorless face showing how deeply she felt the trust.

"I shall hear from you daily?" said Frederick; "you will not neglect to write me? If a lengthened silence should fall on your side, I shall return here at any hazard. It is hard to leave my mother, but absolutely impossible, in her present weak condition, to remove her to a place of safety."

Millicent knew that it was so.

"The doctor will not come again," observed Frederick, dropping his voice, as he glanced into the open chamber. "He has promised instructions; you will have to send for them."

Millicent understood the restriction.

"If any danger should come to your knowledge, do not hesitate to write me at once and fully."

"Your valise be packed, mas'er," called Joe, from the foot of the stairs.

"Very well, Joe; I will be down in a moment."

Frederick took his cousin's hand. Its pulses trembled with the quickness of a fever heat as it lay in his. The excitements of the past night had evidently wrought upon her nerves.

"Good-by, Millicent," he said, in a low voice, not quite free from emotion upon his own part, and, dropping her passive fingers, stepped away.

He went on to take leave of his mother and sister, while Millicent, after turning back to attend to the wants of her patient, stole up to her own chamber to find a few moments by herself. Her window commanded a view of the bend of the road which Frederick must pass; she strained her eyes upon it through the thick foliage to be rewarded in a few moments by a glimpse of two horsemen, — the master and his servant riding rapidly on.

Millicent drew a deep breath as she turned away, and the next instant her face dropped in her hands, while a burning glow suffused her cheek. She had made a discovery for herself an hour ago which a more worldly-learned woman would have made earlier. She could not be thrown daily into the society of her Cousin Frederick, and under such peculiar circumstances as the last few weeks had brought about, without experiencing the attractions of his person and manners. A deep and hopeless attachment had gradually grown up in her heart. If she had but had a mother to warn her; if her aunt had only taken that kind part; but how should she dream of her presumption?

"I must get the better of this," thought Millicent. "It will never do. How I wish he had not asked me to write to him!" She blushed again, this time at her disingenuousness, and stood up before the mirror to arrange her disordered braids. It was a pretty face which the oval glass gave back, quite changed from the wan, sallow girl who had come to Rossenville but a few months back. Health and appreciation work wonders, — the first had tinted the wan complexion with the fairness of the lily; the last had given a deeper light to the really lustrous dark eyes, and changed the whole of that shy, awkward exterior which is the worst enemy to grace. As far as beauty was concerned, Millicent's timid eyes could not deny to herself that she stood a fair chance of winning Mr. Frederick Leeson's heart. He had been kind to her too; had leaned upon her assistance in these hours of peril, and, in his departure, had left to her a most sacred charge; but the disparity of station, still to be got over, was enough in itself to rebuke her ambitious thoughts.

"What shall I do?" murmured the poor girl, dropping her head again.

To quit this place, to begin the struggle to forget him, to leave out of sight

all which could recall him by association,
her judgment told her would be the wisest
plan; but duty held her here, even if necessity had not. She could not leave her
aunt in her helpless condition, or her young
cousin. The unusual circumstances of the
last weeks had reversed her position, and
the relationship which on her coming had
been so coldly ignored stood forth now in
its full force.

"I will do what is before me to do,"
was her sensible thought, "and leave the
issues to God."

She went down to her aunt's chamber
to receive what instructions Mrs. Leeson
might have for her. They were very few.
Her aunt seemed too deeply merged in her
grief at parting with her son to be capable of giving much attention to outward
things. She might rouse from this state
shortly; but Millicent saw that the direction of matters depended at present upon
herself. She did not think it best to acquaint the servants with the very indefi-

nite length of their master's absence, but
rather to place it at a short duration,
which would lessen materially the difficulties to be expected in their management.
That some of them would seize upon the
opportunity now offered to obtain their liberty she had little doubt; and should such
an emergency arise, she felt that her conscience would allow her to throw very few
obstacles in their way. The wounded negro, she soon ascertained, held the part of
Mr. Leeson's overseer, to which his intelligence, not less than his master's favor
had raised him above his comrades, and in
his sickness it was necessary for her to
make a new selection. Here she conde-
scended to ask Dinah's advice, greatly to
the satisfaction of that person.

Under the circumstances, she decided it
to be best for the negroes to return to
their old quarters. If another attack should
be menaced, no resistance could be offered,
and their presence in the house, coupled
with the events of the past night, would,

in such an event, prove a serious cause
of irritation. A share of her attention was
due in the sick-chamber, where she in-
stalled Rose; and late in the afternoon, as
the negro's symptoms continued to grow
steadily worse, she sent Jim to the doctor
for advice and medicine, writing down
carefully a detail of the unfavorable symptoms for his perusal. Perhaps he would
allow himself to be prevailed upon to come
and dress the wound — a service which
she shrank from taking upon herself, as
well from her woman's cowardice as ignorance — when the fact of Mr. Leeson's abrupt departure should get abroad; but of
this she could entertain little hope.

CHAPTER XXXV.

A STOLEN VISIT.

ONE, two, three weeks went by. The family at Wheatley Place began to dismiss their fears, and to fall back in security upon very nearly the old tranquil life. The wounded negro, under Millicent's skilful nursing, grew better, and at the end of July was able to take his place in the field. Mrs. Leeson, relieved of a part of her anxiety, revived sufficiently to leave her bed. Letters came often from Frederick to his sister and cousin, with thoughtful postscripts to his mother, each glowing with the ardor of the soldier, and showing more and more how fully he had thrown his heart into the cause which he had at this late hour espoused.

301

"Frederick was designed for a soldier," observed his mother, laying down one of these hastily-scrawled sheets; "he has found his vocation. God grant," she added, mournfully, "that he may be preserved through these coming battles, and spared a meeting with James."

"There will be a great battle soon," said Adéle, to whom the news of the day had begun to wear an absorbing interest. "Do you know General Polk has taken Columbus? What if his army should advance this way!"

Millicent sat at the open window, holding a letter which Jim had brought her with Mrs. Leeson's. It was from her step-mother. Her eldest son, James, had fallen in the battle of Bethel. A mystery had rested upon his fate for several weeks; but at last it had been mournfully solved, and placed beyond a doubt. A tear fell from Millicent's eye upon the sheet. She thought of the kind-hearted boy who had grown up with her, a frank, manly youth, whose future had shown full of promise. To-day he was lying in a soldier's bloody grave, the spot perhaps unmarked.

"How many more such sacrifices will God require for the sins of our nation?" she pondered, forcing back her tears.

It would not do to disquiet her aunt with her bad news. She put away her letter, and in a few moments, seized an opportunity of retiring by herself to her chamber.

"Be the Union army coming, Miss Halford?" asked Rose, that night, as she lingered a few moments in the kitchen. "Jim says it is, and that it will make us all free."

"Your master is in the Union army, Rose," said Millicent, in a tone of grave reproof.

The dream of liberty had entered into even this thoughtless girl's mind; the hour of fruition might be indeed at hand.

Millicent, with her Christian faith, saw that events were thitherward tending; but her eyes, like ours, were sealed to the frightful waste of blood and treasure which must bring this blessing. It was the old story of Pharaoh, who would not let his bondmen go.

The end of August brought a visit from Frederick, a sudden and quite unexpected event.

It was in the dusk of evening; tea was over. Mrs. Leeson, who had come down-stairs on the previous day for the first time in many weary weeks, sat in her easy-chair by a window. Adéle had stepped out into the garden. Millicent was sitting not far from her aunt, engaged in building one of the quiet air-castles to which she was wont now and then to surrender her silent hours.

A quick, firm step in the hall startled them both from their reveries; the door was flung open, and ere Mrs. Leeson could finish her short exclamation of alarm, she found herself reassured by her son's well-known voice, and the warm clasp of his hand.

"My dear mother, this is indeed pleasant to find you here."

"Oh, Frederick, what has led you to take such a risk? If you should be caught! The neighborhood would be in arms against you, if they should dream of your being here."

"I have no intention of being caught, mother. I came rapidly; I have only three days' furlough, one of which is used up. Millicent, is that you?"

He might well ask. The darkness in the room hid her face; he could discern little more than the outlines of a girlish figure. She came forward to give him her hand. She would not trust herself with a word to add to Mrs. Leeson's already-quickened fears; but the knowledge of his danger made her feel quite faint. She said something about a light, and stepped back to the door opening on the passage which led to the kitchen.

"What ails you, Miss Halford? You are as white as a sheet," said Lizzie, as she went in.

"Lizzie, can you keep a secret?" asked Millicent.

"I tink I can, Miss Millicent. Is it 'bout mas'er?"

"Yes; he has come home; but his life wont be safe for an hour if the neighborhood knows of it. We must keep his being here among ourselves; it wont be for long."

Lizzie entered upon the secrecy required of her with zest; she would answer for her fellow-servants. Millicent ordered a fresh supper to be got, and went back.·

Adéle was sitting on the sofa by her brother as she came in, her arm around his neck. Frederick looked handsome in his fresh uniform.

"We have no visitors," his mother was saying. "I believe all show of neighborhood toward us has been dropped since you left."

A state of things to be expected. The loyalty of James Leeson could preserve his brother's roof over the heads of his helpless mother and young sister when that roof was well known to be under a heavy mort-

gage to the heirs of one of the late incendiary party; but it could not protect them
farther from the excited state of feeling
which had followed upon Frederick's too
successful night resistance.

The tea-bell rang shortly, and Millicent
preceded Frederick out to take her usual
place at the table, and preside at his meal.

"You have spoken for the silence of the
servants, Millicent?" observed Frederick,
helping himself to the freshly-prepared toast
with the hearty appetite which his long day's
fast had engendered.

Millicent wondered how he had guessed
her immediate precaution as she answered
in the affirmative.

"I can count on their fidelity," he remarked, — "on the house servants, at least.
The field hands need not be told. I shall
have to keep close to-morrow, I suppose,
to escape the possibility of a glimpse from
prying eyes."

"You start on your way back to-morrow
night?" queried Millicent.

"Yes, that is the length of my leave of absence,—just a glimpse of you all to assure myself that things are going on as favorably as they are represented in your letters. I did hope"—his voice fell to a slightly-lowered tone—"to make arrangements for my mother's removal, her journey to follow upon mine by easy stages; but I see to-night that my plan cannot be carried out for the present."

"I was wrong," said Millicent, with a pang of self-reproach, "to write you so cheerfully of her improved health; but I understood all your anxieties."

"It has done no harm," returned Mr. Leeson. "I dislike to break in upon my mother's impressions of security; but I fear that she is entirely deceived. I base my opinion on some information received from Miss Bennet, who joined her father at our camp a few days ago."

Millicent looked surprised. She had heard of Mrs. Bennet's death through Dinah, and that the two young children had been sent

North in the charge of a relative; but of Miss Bennet's whereabouts she had no idea, least of all that she had set out for Lexington.

"What is to be apprehended?" she asked, anxiously, as Frederick continued silent. "Certainly this band of wicked men will not war upon helpless women?"

"Their object is to run off my negroes and waste my property," said Frederick. "Reasons which you may be at no loss to guess have led them to hesitate in their plans, and produced a divided state of feeling among them. Without doubt, too, they have counted upon an opportunity like the present, and still hope that, lulled by a false belief of security, I shall commit the imprudence of putting myself in their power."

Millicent shuddered.

"I shall use every precaution," he added, glancing at her disturbed face. "If the secret of my short stay here goes no farther than my family and the house servants, there is hardly a possibility of discovery."

"It would be death to his mother if he should be taken," thought Millicent, trying to put away the selfish picture of herself as she rose to lead the way back to the sitting-room.

CHAPTER XXXVI.

JIM.

MR. LEESON would have entertained a less happy confidence in his security, could he have witnessed a little scene which took place almost in the shadow of the gray, irregular line of out-buildings an hour later, while he sat talking with his sister and Millicent, his mother having just retired to her chamber under the care of Dinah. The moon was at full, and shed a flood of silvery light over the short grass of the lawn, the dew-sprinkled beds of the garden, and the clump of slender sycamores down the walk. Jim, the stable-boy, stood leaning against a tree, in an attitude more suggestive of comfort than of picturesque effect, his eyes strained in the direction of the kitchen windows, in the evident expectation of being joined by some one. Presently the door opposite to him unclosed; a light figure stepped out, and Rose tripped lightly toward him.

"What does you tink, Jim?" she ejaculated, when the first greetings suited to the occasion had passed. "Mas'er Frederick hab got home, — come dis night!"

A sudden gleam of interest flashed up into Jim's bright eyes.

"You hab seen him, Rose?"

"No, Lizzie told me. I saw Joe, too, in de kitchen. Dey is not to hab it told ob dat dey be here."

"De gemmen would be arter Mas'er Frederick if dey knew," said Jim, with a low chuckle.

"'Pears like dey would; but who's to tell ob it?"

Jim glanced up at the out-buildings whose shadow lay dark over the green grass. The reverie into which he was falling made him unconscious for the moment of his companion's presence.

Rose pouted, and pulled coquettishly at the bright-colored shawl which lay over her shoulders.

"I must run back," she said; "Dinah will miss me. She said she had a lot ob work for me to do when she came down from missus' chamber."

Jim made no attempt to detain her, but followed her graceful movements with his eyes as she glided across, and disappeared through the lighted door.

Jim had not forgotten his whipping, administered first at the direction of his mistress, and on the second occasion under the orders of his master, Mr. Frederick Leeson. The degradation of the lash had burned itself into his soul. Its first stroke upon his bare shoulders had put to flight every sentiment of affection toward the family in which he had been reared. Very likely he would have seized upon the opportunity afforded by his master's absence to attempt a second plan of escape, this time with more sanguine hopes of success; but a mag-

net held him back, to whose attractions all
of us are more or less susceptible. He
could not leave Rose; she timidly shrank
from becoming the companion of his flight,
and though the subject had been twice or
thrice broached between them, he had as
yet made little progress in overcoming her
fears. If overtaken and brought back, she
well knew that even her sex could not save
her under her mistress' hands from the
cruel punishment of the lash. She drew
many a wistful sigh over the golden-tinted
picture of liberty which Jim's eager tongue
painted; but she, poor thing, had not the
courage to take the risk.

The demon of revenge wrestled for mas-
tery in Jim's breast as he stood under the
shadow of the tree, his eyes turned now
from the blazing kitchen windows to the
more tempered light which stole out through
a displaced curtain in the sitting-room beyond, glistening over the wet vines which
twined around the pillars of the veranda.
He saw in imagination the cheerful picture

inside. What sympathy had he with it, a
slave? He took a step forward, a heavy
frown darkening his face. A few paces beyond would take him within the range of
the window; he could satisfy his own
sight.

The vines lay thick around the white
pillars, the moonlight shimmering over their
glossy leaves. The low windows were
open, and voices stole outside. His quick
ear was at no loss to recognize his master's.
He crept closer, the soft turf burying his
steps.

Frederick had resumed his seat on the
sofa on his re-entrance from the dining-
room, and the full profile of his face confronted the window. His young sister,
Adéle, was beside him, her countenance
beaming with smiles. Miss Halford sat at
a little distance, her hands lying in her lap,
her face clouded with an anxious expression
whenever she looked up at Mr. Leeson.
Mrs. Leeson's vacant easy-chair showed that
she had retired.

A stern, cruel gleam shot over the negro's face as he crouched down, peering stealthily in. All his struggling purposes were confirmed at the sight of his master; he no longer hesitated upon his course.

Creeping back with the same stealthy tread which had borne him up to the window, Jim stole down the edge of the carriage-path and stepped into the road. He showed no hesitation as to his course, but struck out directly for the house of a near neighbor, whose strong political proclivities he had on more than one occasion overheard discussed by his master's guests. He had, in fact, shared in the former unfortunate night attack on Mr. Leeson's dwelling, and came off with a slight wound on the occasion, which fact, though he had at the time taken some prudent pains to suppress it, was the property of the neighborhood.

Thither Jim shaped his way, and gave a modest knock at the door of the back entrance.

The woman who came to the door recognized him as one of the servants at Wheatley Place, and regarded him with some surprise. Mr. Rawdon was in, she said; but what was Jim's errand? Mas'er wouldn't want to be disturbed for nothing.

Jim replied that his errand was of the greatest importance, and that he must see Mas'er Rawdon at once.

The woman went in and presently came out saying that he had retired to bed sick, and could not be seen for the night.

Here was a difficulty for Jim to get over; but his genius proved equal to the emergency. He repeated that his errand was "ob de bery last importance," and he would take upon himself dat Mas'er Rawdon would not be displeased if he was shown up to his chamber.

The woman went back, and presently returned, telling Jim to follow her.

Mr. Rawdon lay in bed, groaning with a severe headache, and in a state of mind somewhat unpropitious for the reception of his visitor.

"What brings you here, you black rascal?" he began. "Out with your errand, and be quick over it."

"Mas'er Frederick is home, sar," said Jim, dropping his voice to a tone befitting the importance of his communication.

"The devil he is!" exclaimed the sick man, starting up on his elbow,—"and he sent you over to tell me, did he?"

"No, mas'er; I crept off. He's just come."

Mr. Rawdon lay back, and began to gather the clothes over him, his face working with excitement. "How long is he going to stay, Jim?" he asked.

Jim, as the reader knows, had received no information upon this point; but it did not suit his dignity to appear ignorant. "Two days, mas'er; he can't get off for a longer time dan dat."

"How unlucky!" muttered Rawdon, running over a sudden train of thought. "Delford is out of the way, so is Fouchard. This cursed headache ties me here. Jim,"

he added, speaking aloud, " be you sure of
the length of your master's visit?"

"Sure as de gospel, mas'er," responded
Jim, with an honest air of indignation at
being doubted.

"He's paying an old grudge, no doubt,
this nigger," soliloquized Mr. Rawdon from
under the bed-clothes. "This shows what
comes of Leeson's fooling his niggers."

Jim had finished his errand, and after
shuffling awkwardly with his feet in the
pause, turned toward the door. Mr. Rawdon
arrested him as he put his hand on the
latch. "We will pay your master a visit
before long," he said. "Couldn't you contrive to let us in, — say at a proper hour
to-morrow night?"

"I sleeps in de stable-loft, mas'er."

"That settles the question then; but
couldn't you contrive to hide away in the
house?"

"I darsn't risk it, mas'er. Old Dinah, she
be eberywhere."

Mr. Rawdon considered, holding his visitor
by an imperative gesture to the door.

The pain in his head had lulled for a moment under the shock of the exciting intelligence of Mr. Frederick Leeson's return, to resume its seat, as all such paroxysms do, when the first start was over.

"If you could depend upon one of your fellow-servants," he said. "Haven't you a friend you could trust in the house?"

Jim thought of Rose; but he was very sure she would not be equal to the emergency. "I'll do de best I can, mas'er," he ventured.

"Very well, and let us know. To-morrow night it is. We will be on hand at twelve. I wouldn't mind giving you a handsome present, my good fellow, if you will help us to carry this out without risk."

Jim's eyes brightened, and his lips parted, displaying two pearly rows of ivory. Mr. Rawdon had his man, — at least, he thought so; but the wisest of us will fall into mistakes. Money was not Jim's passion; revenge and liberty were just now the dearest matters in his consideration.

He would have been incapable of selling his master, slave as he was, for the thirty pieces of silver, much less for promises whose worthlessness his quick wit no doubt detected. He bowed a respectful good-night to Mr. Rawdon, and took himself out.

21

CHAPTER XXXVII.

JIM AND ROSE.

IT was a quiet walk home in the moonlight. Jim quickened his steps, keeping a stealthy eye on the open road as well as the clumps of bushes which here and there flowered along the highway, and had the good fortune to turn into his master's carriage-path without having encountered a solitary pedestrian. He reached the shadow of the stable buildings, and flung himself down lazily on the wet grass, surrendering himself to a fit of profound reflection. It was his purpose to get away in the confusion which would follow on to-morrow night's attack. Rose, of course, would be his companion. The consideration to follow was how he should shape his course. He had little knowledge of the country. To venture into a railroad train without a pass would be certain destruction. He could only do what other poor fugitives had done before him, — keep on in whatever course accident might open. In this instance there would be no pursuit to fear, no harrying with bloodhounds, or flaring advertisement setting forth, with frightful distinctness, his appearance, and offering a bounty to the first man who would restore him, alive or dead; but all the danger lay in the curiosity of the people he might meet along his route, and in the difficulty of gaining direction toward those friendly Northern cities to which all his hopes culminated.

The light flickered and disappeared from the sitting-room; the family were in the act of retiring to their beds; it was not far from midnight. Jim roused himself from his recumbent position, and betook himself to his quarters in the stable. The tired-out horses which had borne his master and his fellow-servant on their perilous journey of return had been turned into a neighboring pasture, after a liberal supply of grain, furnished under the favorable darkness. As Jim had anticipated, no tokens of Mr. Leeson's arrival presented themselves in the outbuildings.

Jim climbed up the ladder to his usual quarters, and composed himself to sleep on the soft hay. He must see Rose early in the morning, the only part of the day in which an uninterrupted interview could be procured, and confide to her the personal part of his plans; with the whole he dared not trust her. It would be easy to work upon her fears by the intimation of another sale, in which she might expect to be included, and so to force her tardy consent to flight. Jim turned over this last plan very industriously in his mind, and fell asleep just at the moment of its completion.

It was broad daylight when Jim awoke; the sun was shining cheerily through the chinks in the stable. His toilet was already made; he had only to hurry down the ladder, emerge from the open door, and send his scrutinizing glance in the direction of the kitchen.

The dew lay in a shower of brilliants over the grass; the air was fresh and sweet. A female figure, early as was the hour, was flitting about among the beds of the garden, gathering a choice bouquet for the breakfast-room. Of course, the kitchen was astir. A thick smoke was ascending from its slender chimney. Lizzie came to the door for air, with a kettle in her hand. Rose appeared at the window.

Jim sent a quick, magnetic gesture over to her, and presently the young girl came tripping out at the door and over the wet grass toward him.

Jim purposely kept his place, to be out of ear-shot of the house, and even drew her a step or two back after him out of sight of the garden.

"Mas'er be going to sell us, Rose," he said, in a low voice. "Dat's his errand home."

The poor girl clasped her hands with a faint cry, the smiles dying away from her lips. "Be you sure, Jim?" she asked, breathlessly. "Who told you?"

"Somebody dat knew," said Jim, shaking his head. "Missus be going away, and mas'er has bargained to sell us all off but Dinah."

The story was plausible. It did not enter into Rose's innocent faith to doubt it; she had caught snatches of her master's conversation with Millicent at the supper-table the past night, which strengthened her belief. Her mistress was about to be taken away, and, of course, the household would be broken up. A sale must follow. Her face dropped in her hands with a bitter cry.

"Hush!" said Jim, putting his hand on her head. "It's no good taking on so; besides, I's got a plan. We'll run off."

Rose shuddered; it was the last alternative, and to her timid spirit held very little hope.

"De driber wont be 'long 'fore to-morrow morning," said Jim; "we'll take de road to-night. Maybe, if de gemmen knew mas'er was in de neighborhood, dey would pay him a visit; den he would hab enough to do widout looking after us."

"Oh, I darsn't take de risk," said Rose, sobbing; "we shall be caught."

Jim drew himself up with a contemptuous smile, "Rader go off wid de driber? Tell you what, Rose, liberty is worth de risk ob someting."

"But we shall be caught."

"That's jest like you, Rose. Susan got off; why shouldn't we?"

Rose wiped her eyes. "I dunno," she said. "Susan was white; nobody would 'spect her."

"Rose, Rose!" called a voice from the kitchen-door.

"Dat's Lizzie," said the girl, starting, with a quick glance across. "I must run, Jim; I'm wanted. Oh, what shall we do? Missus will see I'm in trouble."

"Keep close, Rose; don't tell Lizzie; mind what I tells you."

Rose was gone, and Jim turned leisurely
back to the stable to his morning work.
The field hands were going to their labors;
the sun had been up an hour. Joe did not
make his appearance out of doors; he had
been over to groom and fodder his horses
with the first glimmer of daylight, and
was now keeping close in obedience to his
master's instructions.

Jim indulged himself in a low whistle as
he set about his work; he had few doubts
of the success of his enterprise.

The day stole away heavily indoors. It
held one or two golden hours for Millicent;
but for the most part a feverish anxiety
pressed upon her spirits. Mrs. Leeson
seemed to be lulled by the influence of her
son's presence into a strange lethargy of
security.

Twilight came on. Mrs. Leeson, yielding
to fatigue, despite her first resolution to
sit up till the hour of her son's departure,
retired to her chamber, where Dinah had
preceded her. Her maid seemed in a state

of unusual depression, and gave but brief replies to her mistress' monosyllabic inquiries touching household matters. Presently she relieved her mind.

"Rose is taking on bad to-day, missus. Jim says we servants are going to be sold."

"One of Jim's stories," said her mistress, yawning. "Here, these pillows are all in a heap. Can't you fix them properly, Dinah? Wake me, if I should drop asleep, when Frederick comes in."

Blind, blind! How could her ear be so dull to the warning?

CHAPTER XXXVIII.

THE ALARM.

THE hours were deepening toward midnight; the clock was upon the stroke of eleven; a full moon was shining out of doors. Joe had brought round the horses to the winding carriage-path, where they stood huddled in the friendly shade of the growth of sycamores. Frederick stood in the hall holding his cousin's hand; he had just come down from his mother's chamber. Adéle had said her good-by, and was crouched down at the foot of the staircase, struggling bravely to keep back a few truant tears.

Millicent could not trust her voice to frame a word. Frederick tried to shake off the spell of foreboding which hung over

him. He had reasons enough for sadness,—
his mother's feeble health, the unprotected
circumstances in which he was leaving these
helpless women, with the perils into which
he was himself hastening.

"Adieu," he said, dropping Millicent's
hand. "I shall write you by the first post.
God keep and preserve you all till we
meet again."

Was she wrong in believing, under her
downcast lashes, that his parting glance
sought hers, or that his fingers had trembled an instant before as they loosed their
clasp? Trifles to build upon; but trifles
are everything in love.

The door closed noiselessly after him;
he had passed out into the moonlight. Adéle
ran into the sitting-room to catch a parting
glimpse from the veranda. Millicent mechanically followed her, saw the horsemen mount,
caught at the distance a parting wave of
the hand from the taller of the two, whose
quick eye had distinguished the flutter of
their white garments among the vines

around the porch, and saw them canter out into the road.

All was still, — a deep, oppressive stillness. A bird disturbed in the bushes close by sent up suddenly a low chirp. The two women turned indoors. Millicent went up straight to her chamber. Adéle lingered at the door of her mother's room, to see if she were still waking.

Two minutes later Jim stole out from the stable with a small bundle in his hand, containing his little suit of worldly goods, and made up to the veranda. The lights were gone from the sitting-room; he had made sure of this from a chink in the stable. Rose had promised to meet him as soon as the family should have retired, and the house settled to stillness. He crept up to the first window, and laid his ear to the sill. Rose was already there to meet him, a little bundle in her hand, her face swollen with weeping, her spirits at this last moment very uneven and undecided. Jim drew her out, purposely left the sash open after him.

and stepped into the shadow of the vines, hesitating to cross the broad space which spread before them in the full tide of moonlight. Adéle's chamber was situated at that corner of the house. In the excitement attending upon her brother's visit, the young girl might be wakeful and might not yet have retired.

"Miss Adéle be up in missus' room," whispered Rose, guessing at the cause of her lover's hesitation. "She be talking wid missus as I crept by."

Jim brought out an impatient groan. It was not worth while to run the risk of detection in the outset; they had no choice but to wait.

A full half-hour crept on; they dared not trust their voices above a whisper in the close neighborhood of the house. Rose, indeed, was ill-inclined for conversation, and Jim's anxieties on his part left little room for speech. Just as he had made up his mind that his young mistress must have retired, leaving the way clear, and was in the act of arousing his companion, the muffled tread of footfalls came distinctly to his ear. He turned his eyes with a start in the direction of the carriage-path, and saw half a dozen figures stealthily gliding up its outskirts in the direction of the house. These were his master's midnight visitors. He put his hand over Rose's mouth, muffling her cry of alarm, and directed her in a whisper to find her way off the veranda. All the inmates of the household must be wrapped in slumber at this weird hour. She might cross under eye-shot of her master's window without much danger of discovery, and get to the rear of the apple orchard, where he would presently join her.

Rose obeyed him, trembling with a new terror, and by an instinctive movement, rather than any act of conscious volition, reached the designated spot.

Jim was about to follow, when a tall shadow fell over the boards before him, and his affrighted upward glance recognized Mr. Rawdon.

"So you are here, my good fellow," said the gentleman, speaking in a whisper which sounded frightfully distinct in the stillness. "Is the house open? Have we got a friend inside?"

Jim pointed to the window, and made a quick gesture to move away.

"Not so fast," said the visitor, laying his hand heavily on his shoulder; "you must pilot us in, and show us up to your master's chamber."

"Oh, no, mas'er!" said Jim, falling on his knees; "de way's straight 'nuff, —jest up de staircase. I dunno mas'er's room; b'lieve it's to de left or right."

"We will soon find out," said Rawdon, roughly, giving him a shake. "Come, you rascal, if there's any play about this, you'll soon get daylight through your head. Here, Delford, Jones, — this way; the nigger will pilot us. Here, sir, get through the window."

Jim saw that there was no escape. With a cold perspiration starting from every pore, and standing out in great drops on his forehead, he crept in. Close behind him came three or four men, their pistols in their hands, a look of scowling malignity on each of the rough faces.

Jim knew that his life was in the balance with his fidelity, and setting his teeth close, he made a cautious movement up the staircase. One by one they followed, and each gained noiselessly the landing.

Here Jim stopped in some trepidation. The door to the left was certainly his master's. It was not locked, or close shut, but stood slightly ajar. At this point Jim's courage failed him. With a low ejaculation of " Dis be Mas'er Frederick's room," he made a bound back to the head of the staircase, without waiting to see what was to follow. His sudden spring overturned the hindmost of the visitors, whose pistol went off in the confusion, while the three others rushed into the chamber in the hope of still securing their prey in the first moment of surprise.

The room was empty ! The second glance told the story that the bed had not been slept in.

A smothered oath broke from the lips of the foremost, repeated in a variety of voices by the others.

" The nigger has made a mistake !" burst out Mr. Rawdon; " this is the wrong chamber. Quick, men, scatter ! We'll have him yet; but he'll be roused up with this hubbub."

22

CHAPTER XXXIX.

THE HORRORS OF CIVIL WAR.

MRS. LEESON, aroused from her first sleep by the sharp report of a pistol, started up on her elbow with a quick exclamation to her maid, Dinah, already awake, roused up from her recumbent position on the strip of carpet at her mistress' bedside. Both listened, and heard distinctly the footsteps and smothered voices in the passage.

A rude hand pushed open the door of the dressing-room, and a face intruded upon the two terrified women.

"This is one of the women's chambers," said the intruder, speaking to his comrade behind him. "We can get some information out of this negress. Here, you black wench, which is Mr. Leeson's room?"

"My son is not here," said Mrs. Leeson, commanding her terror to speak. "What do you want? If plunder, here is my watch, and all the money I have is in this secretary."

"Money is not our object, madam," said the man, who, in the uncertain light, had failed to distinguish the figure on the bed, and who seemed to be the head of the enterprise. "We want your son."

"He is not here," returned Mrs. Leeson, her voice hardly articulate from fright, and driven by the pressure of terror into a falsehood; "he has not been here."

"Then that lying nigger shall swing for it," muttered Mr. Rawdon, taking himself out; "but we'll have a search and make good your word for it first, madam."

A fruitless search it proved. His men shortly issued from the upper regions bearing three prisoners with them, — Millicent, Adéle, and Lizzie. The first two ladies — even Adéle, child as she was — preserved a dignified silence to the few short words of questioning put to them; but the terrified negro servant stood ready to confess to anything and everything.

"Mas'er be jest gone," she said; "he habn't been gone clean 'bove an hour."

Millicent threw at her a glance of troubled reproach, which Lizzie, with her face bent down upon her hands, and her whole body shaking with alarm, failed to meet.

"What road did he take?" asked Rawdon, breathlessly; but the woman was unable to answer.

"We'll soon find a way to open your mouths," said Rawdon, in a savage tone, "or you shall see this old roof-tree burning over your heads! Come. here's your choice, — put us on Mr. Leeson's track, or clear out of the house what few movables you can. We'll give you twenty minutes." He took out his watch.

Millicent turned pale; Adéle wrung her hands with a terrified gesture.

"I don't believe he's got off at all," continued one of the men; "he's hiding somewhere about in this house."

"The flames will bring him out then," said their leader, shortly.

"Mr. Leeson is not here," said Millicent, struggling to speak. "He is out of your reach; you cannot do him any harm. Certainly, gentlemen, you will not war upon helpless women!"

"You waste time, ma'am," said one of the men. "You'd better be about clearing the house."

"Yes," said their leader, "we shall put the torch at the end of the twenty minutes."

They scattered as by one impulse in pursuit of plunder, leaving the two girls at the door of Mrs. Leeson's chamber. Lizzie had crouched down upon the floor, and was sobbing helplessly in her terror.

"What will become of mamma?" whispered Adéle. "Poor mamma! she will get her death in this damp night."

At this instant, to their dismay, Mrs. Leeson appeared in the door, having been hurriedly dressed by Dinah. The excitement of the hour had given her strength, and

she had come out to join her feeble petition
to that of the two trembling girls before
her that these midnight visitors would re-
spect the sanctity of her home.

They found Mr. Rawdon in an adjoining
chamber in the act of curiously inspecting
the closets, no doubt in the forlorn hope
of still discovering the object of his search.
The women surrounded him with passionate entreaties to revoke his hasty order.

" It's no use," he answered, savagely.
" You'd better stop your crying, and clear
the house. You are only wasting time."

It was plain that it was so. Mrs. Leeson
sunk down fainting in a chair. Adéle ran
to support her mother, while Millicent hurried out for a glass of water.

"We must get out the carriage," thought
the poor girl, " if I can only find Jim. What
is to be saved? Where shall we get shelter?"

She aroused Lizzie, administered a hearty
shaking to awaken her from her fright, and
placing the glass of water in her hand,

bade her go to her mistress. She stopped
to see that, in her bewilderment, the girl
had not missed her way, and then proceeded down the staircase. She had not far to
go in her search, but quickly discovered
Jim in the custody of the two men who
had been left to keep guard outside. They
were amusing themselves with their pris-
oner, with the utterance of various threats
to be carried out in the case of his master's non-discovery, which came to an abrupt
pause at her appearance. Millicent hesitated, undecided what to do.

"You will let us take out the carriage?"
she said, addressing one of the men. "Mrs.
Leeson is hardly able to leave her chamber; it will be sure death to her to be
turned out on foot in this damp night."

They looked at each other in uncertainty.
Mrs. Leeson was a sick, helpless old woman
who had done nothing to offend them. One
of her sons was in the Confederate army;
she was not answerable for the other's
politics. Jim was set at liberty, and pro-

ceeded with alacrity to turn out the two carriage horses.

Millicent went back to give orders to Dinah, and to gather up her own scanty wearing apparel as rapidly as she might. There was no time to get out the plate, or many other valuable articles which must be left to the flames, should they escape the cupidity of the plunderers. She called out Adéle, leaving Mrs. Leeson to the care of Lizzie, whose terror would have prevented her from proving of any efficient help, and ran up to her chamber.

Ten, fifteen minutes flew by rapidly. Rawdon's rough voice called from the foot of the staircase, " Come, ladies, the twenty minutes are up. We haven't any more time to waste."

The trunks were pushed down with Dinah's strong assistance. Mrs. Leeson followed, leaning heavily on her daughter's arm, whose agitation seemed to render her almost incapable of her own support. Lizzie, with a small bundle hastily crowded together, brought up the rear.

It was a sorrowful picture; but no pity-ing moisture shone in the scowling eyes which watched it. They went out at the hall-door and stood on the veranda, from which Millicent and Adéle had watched Frederick's departure, and met his last parting salutation, little more than an hour before.

"Thank God! *he* is safe," whispered Mil-licent, pressing her aunt's arm. "Let us take courage."

Mrs. Leeson replied only by a groan. Her eyes turned beseechingly to Mr. Raw-don, who had followed the mournful com-pany out, and waited to see them off. "Oh, sir, have pity!" she exclaimed. "You have a mother. Think what it is to have an old woman turned out of doors!"

"It is a hard case, ma'am," said the gen-tleman addressed. "Your son should have had thought for you."

The carriage and horses appeared at the opening of the carriage-path, but without a driver. Jim had seized a favorable moment to skedaddle, and taken himself securely out of sight and hearing. Here was a dilemma. No one knew in what direction to go, if the trunks could be got on, and the horses started. Mrs. Leeson was quite past giving directions. Millicent found again that the weight of authority must rest upon her hands. She recalled a log-house about a mile distant, whose owner had received several favors at her aunt's hands. She might be persuaded to shelter them for the present in their homeless condition. For Mrs. Leeson to accomplish a journey of much distance in her present state, not to consider the damp air of midnight, which was already sending a shiver through her slender frame, was impossible.

The trunks were got on with the united exertions of the little group, Mrs. Leeson was helped in, and Millicent took the reins. A backward glance showed the negro quarters open and deserted. The negroes had early taken the alarm, and scattered into the fields.

The horses started at an easy pace. Mrs. Leeson dropped her head with a low, heart-wrung sob. Adéle leaned out of the carriage window for one last farewell look at the old home which was soon to lie in a heap of crumbling cinders. "Oh, if Fred. were here," she exclaimed, passionately, "with his company of men! Oh, mother, if he could only have known of this!"

"Thank God," repeated Millicent, gently, turning her face, "that *he* is safe. We can bear everything with that!"

CHAPTER XL.

THE NIGHT DRIVE.

THEY had proceeded about half a mile when a flaming light rose up in the sky behind them, starting the horses from their even pace, and calling out all Millicent's care and skill in their management. Broader and broader it grew till the whole heavens were overspread, and the little party distinctly heard the roaring of the flames and the sharp crack of the parting timbers, in the still night air. Dinah ground her teeth with a smothered ejaculation, "The debils are having their time." Adéle's eyes kindled, their light the next instant drenched in a flood of tears. Mrs. Leeson crouched back closer in her corner of the carriage. Lizzie's sobs broke out anew. The old

348

homestead was fast falling into a sheet of red flame. The vines around the veranda, the flowers in the little garden, — but yesterday morning so fresh, — were shrivelling in the hot heat, and over it all demons, in human shape, were gloating in the triumph of revenge.

The horses were fast growing unmanageable. Millicent, whose thoughts had turned from the burning buildings to centre around the safety of her companions, began to be sensible of an emotion of terror. A tall hill rose at a short distance before her. If she could slacken their pace up the ascent, all would be well; if not, she trembled at the thought of the headlong plunge which might threaten on the other side. Exerting all her strength, she drew in the reins tightly, and tried to curb the alarmed steeds with her voice. The steady horses gradually relaxed into a slackened run, and to her great relief, allowed themselves to be brought to an abrupt stop at the foot of the ascent. It was an open country, with

a wide margin of stubble land on each side
of the road, and a broad line of what appeared to be thick woods spreading away
at a little distance to the right.

"Where shall we go, Millicent?" asked
Adéle, clinging to her cousin's dress to
draw her attention. "Mamma cannot go
much farther. See how ill she looks!"

Millicent did not need to turn her face
to catch her aunt's woe-begone aspect. The
humble log-hut which had first come to
her thoughts was but a few yards distant;
it would appear in sight on mounting the
hill. She whispered a few words to Adéle,
and again started the horses, this time at
a slow pace.

The slope at the foot of the hill brought
her to her destination; it was a small clearing on the outskirts of the wood, occupied
by a rude log-house, a vegetable garden in
front, rudely fenced with rough pine boards.

Millicent got out, tethered her horses with
some difficulty to a tree, and proceeded to
arouse the inmates of the dwelling by a

vigorous succession of knocks bestowed with the end of her whip.

Presently a night-capped head was thrust out the window, the coarse cotton ruffle surrounding a labor-seamed but honest woman's face.

"And what be you after wanting at this time o' night?" was her Hibernian salutation.

"You know us, Mrs. Brown," said Millicent, approaching the window. "Mrs. Leeson, of Wheatley Place, is in this carriage. We have been turned out of our house, and have come to beg of you a night's shelter."

"Bless my soul!" said the woman, looking up at the sky, which presented a crimson glare overhead. "There's a great fire somewhere, and it isn't far off either. The regulators are to work again. Arrah, sorry times these for some folks!"

Two curly heads protruded out of the window at the first sentence at their mother's side, curiously taking in the flaming aspect of the sky, and wandering from that to the strange spectacle of the equipage halting a few paces from their door.

"Will you give us shelter?" repeated Millicent, anxiously. "Mrs. Leeson is very feeble; I fear she cannot get much farther."

"Yes, my dear. What am I thinking of? It's the fire that's quite dazed me;" and Mrs. Brown hurried to the door, drew out the creaking bolt, and opened it wide for the admission of her visitors. "It's your own house thin that's burning!" she ejaculated. "Sorry comforts I can offer to such a lady; but the best I have is for her, and she's welcome."

Millicent did not stop to hear her courtesies; she was at the side of the carriage whispering to Adéle to assist her mother to alight. The young lady threw a discontented glance at the poor place, and hesitated to descend. "We can do no more," whispered Millicent; "every other door would be shut to us; this poor woman alone runs no danger."

Adéle submitted with a sigh, and getting
out, prepared to assist her mother to descend. Mrs. Leeson's nervous strength was
fast succumbing under exhaustion; she
reached the house with some exertion, and
sunk into the chair which her hostess hurried to place for her. The inner part of
the log-house proved to consist of but one
room, partially divided by a curtain. Mrs.
Brown cheerfully gave up her bed to Mrs.
Leeson, and the little party set about making themselves as comfortable as their peculiar circumstances would admit.

"We have relatives at Belmont," said
Adéle to her cousin, in a whisper, as they
sat together an hour after their arrival, —
Mrs. Brown had considerately withdrawn to
the opposite part of the house, leaving her
guests to themselves, — "if mamma could
only get there."

"She will die here," said Millicent, glancing with a shudder around the bare walls.
"The effort must certainly be made, even
if we are obliged to return with her."

23

CHAPTER XLI.

THE BATTLE OF BELMONT.

IT was the night following the 9th of November. The battle of Belmont was over; the victorious Union forces had taken up a line of retreat to their gunboats, and the friendly twilight was beginning to veil the mournful scenes of death and suffering which followed close upon the roar and smoke of conflict. In an open field on the outskirts of the village where the struggle had raged the fiercest, lay a heap of mangled forms in which life seemed to be utterly extinct, with one or two still breathing figures stretched on the stubble earth beside them. One of these wore the uniform of a Confederate officer of some rank, which was still discernible in the

354

dusk; the other, by his blue coat, was a Union private, who most likely had been left for dead in the hurried departure of his comrades. Both were young, of such materials as enter most into the mass of armies, in the flower and vigor of life.

"Will no one come?" groaned the officer, turning up a despairing look at the sky. "It is horrible to think of lying here all night, within a few yards of friends, and suffering, too, with this intolerable thirst!"

Even as he spoke a light footfall broke the stillness near them, and two female figures, their sex distinguishable by a mass of light drapery, came with hesitating footfalls over the ground toward them. The foremost, who was a few rods in advance of her companion, stopped at the heap of corpses on the knoll, and, conquering her trembling repugnance, began to bend over them. A low, bitter cry instantly burst from her lips. "Oh, Fanny, he is here! I knew it would be so. O God!" She sunk down upon the grass, wringing her hands, and rocking herself to and fro with a low succession of sobs. Her companion went up to her and put her arm around her neck, as if to draw her away.

"Come," she said, her voice showing that she was shivering from head to foot, "we will go and get assistance to have him carried to the house. Come, Jane, this is a horrible spot, and it's not safe to linger here; it's growing dark."

The sobbing woman started up, and put her hand upon her companion's arm.

"Ladies," said the wounded officer, as they turned to move away, "will you give me some water? I and this poor fellow here are dying of thirst."

The women started at a voice near them. Their first movement seemed to be to flee; but the woman who had knelt over the dead body gently restrained her companion.

"We will send help to you," she said, "and have you taken into a house. I thought all the wounded had been carried away."

She did not ask, true to her woman's sympathies, to which side the wounded man belonged, but quickened her steps to a rapid walk in the direction of the houses.

Major James Leeson — for the wounded officer was no other than this gentleman — laid his head back again wearily on the hard ground, and surrendered himself to await with what patience he could the amelioration of his condition. His comrade beside him had relapsed into a second faint, and lay quite unconscious of anything around him, with the blood congealed at his side from a hideous wound in his breast. The stars were coming out thickly in the blue sky overhead; a reviving night breeze blew over the fields; the wounded man struggled with his feverish impatience.

By and by, after what seemed an age of space, his ear caught distinctly the tread of footsteps coming out of the distance, and shortly two men, bearing a rough litter, hastily formed of two wooden slabs, and preceded by a female figure, carrying a lantern, halted beside him.

"This is the spot," said a low voice, which sounded strangely familiar, though his senses were beginning to grow weak with the pain and loss of blood following his wound.

"One. of them is quite gone," said one of the men, bending over his blue-coated comrade. "See! his eyes are set."

James tried to lift his head, to assist his bearers to raise him to the litter; but the exertion proved too much. A sudden faintness came over him, and his eyes closed just as the lantern slipped from the relaxing fingers of the guide with a low ejaculation of his name.

When Mr. Leeson returned to consciousness, he found himself lying on a bed in a large, airy chamber. It was broad daylight; the sun was shining cheerily through an aperture in the displaced curtain, and the wintry branches of a naked tree drew his attention outside. As he lay, thoughtful and conscious, he became aware that a long interval must have elapsed since the night of his wound, and that he was now in-debted to the charity of some kind friend, who had nursed him through his delirium, instead of the chary attentions doled out at a hospital. Two or three figures who had held no small share in his fever-col-ored fancies flitted distinctly before his memory. He was quite sure that a famil-iar presence had more than once penetrated to his bedside, and that he had heard his name pronounced by the same lips which had faltered it in the twilight when he sunk down fainting — as he then thought dying — on the cold ground.

"You are awake, sir," observed a quiet voice from the depths of the easy-chair at his bedside. "Will you take your medi-cine now?" Mr. Leeson looked up to see a wrinkled, kindly-looking face, in a close widow's cap, with black bands, bending over him.

"Is it a narcotic, ma'am?" he asked, hesitating to swallow the contents of the glass which was placed to his lips.

"I don't know, sir; the doctor said it was a soothing draught."

"I should like to ask a question or two first," said the patient. "Where am I? and who has so kindly taken care of me in my sickness?"

"You are still in the village of Belmont, sir. The family you are with is named Anson. You were brought here insensible on the night of the battle."

"Ah, I remember." Mr. Leeson put his hand feebly to his temples. "I think we were masters of the field at the last?"

"It was a drawn battle, sir," said the old lady, discreetly steering between the rival claims of the victory. "The Union forces drew off in good order, and your side was left in possession of the field. But the doctor said you were not to talk when you should come to yourself. Be pleased to swallow your medicine."

"One more question, my good lady. How long have I been lying here?"

"Close upon three weeks, sir."

Major Leeson repressed a groan. What had become of his command? Did his comrades believe him dead? Most likely they did, since he had been passed over by them in an obscure spot upon the field.

"You had better try to sleep, and get ugly thoughts out of your head, sir," said his nurse, watching his face. "The doctor said worrying would retard your getting up."

Certainly some friendly care was near him. Mr. Leeson swallowed the nauseous draught, laid his head back on his pillow, and resigned himself to his situation.

Presently a deep, refreshing slumber stole over him, and the old nurse, rising on tiptoe, glided noiselessly out of the chamber.

CHAPTER XLII.

RETROSPECTION.

MAJOR LEESON'S convalescence was rapid. On the fourth day he was able to quit his bed for a lounge placed opposite a window which commanded a wide view of the surrounding country; but with his improvement in strength his docility as a patient lapsed, and he began to press his kind nurse with inquiries on a point which deeply excited his curiosity. Was it the illusion of a fever dream which painted, on two or three occasions, a fair face bathed in tears at his pillow, or which distinctly treasured up the pressure of a hand, too small and ·soft to belong to his withered nurse, in more than one heated night of delirium, upon his temples?

362

"I have a distinct impression of hearing a familiar voice on the night in which I was taken up from the field," he said to his nurse. "Good Mrs. Anson, will you not have pity upon my fever-clouded brain, and set me right?"

"The lady who found you was Miss Bennet," said Mrs. Anson, answering with reluctance. "She was in search of her father's body; he fell in the beginning of the action. I believe they were old neighbors of yours?"

"Yes," said Mr. Leeson, turning away his face. "But how came she here?" he asked, after a pause. "The family are still at Rossenville?"

"Her mother is dead," said Mrs. Anson, in a tone which betrayed surprise at the very meagre extent of her questioner's knowledge. "She got her death from the exposure following upon her being turned out of doors by a party of regulators, who burned up her house."

"It was sad!" Major Leeson could

afford to sympathize with this personal case, —the misfortunes of his late lady-love.

"The children were sent North," pursued Mrs. Anson. "Miss Bennet has been staying here for the last few weeks."

Mr. Leeson closed his eyes, quite exhausted by the shock of the information he had just received. Jane Bennet was an orphan, suddenly left without friends or means in the world. Of course, her father's unlucky stand in politics had sequestered his property. He, Mr. Leeson, owed his life to her; for no common care could have carried him safely through these three weeks of fever. A hot glow shot up to his temples as he thought of it.

"Will you ask Miss Bennet to come in and see me?" he said, an hour later, as his nurse rose to leave him alone. "We are old friends; and I should like, beside, to express my sense of these obligations."

It would prove an embarrassing meeting under any circumstances, but better carried out in the weakness of this still languid

convalescence than at a later period of fuller
health. He lay back on the lounge, waiting with an impatience which seemed
strange to himself the approach of the
well-remembered footstep. He waited in
vain, and presently the nurse reappeared,
saying that Miss Bennet would see him on
the morrow. "She leaves us in a few
days," she added. "I believe she has applied for a situation as assistant nurse in
some hospital."

Mr. Leeson turned his face languidly upon his pillow; he was surprised at the
feeling of disappointment which oppressed
him. What were Jane Bennet's plans to
him? Certainly nothing.

Another matter should have claimed a
share in Mr. Leeson's thoughts, and certainly did for the next few minutes. It
was his purpose to pen a note to Augusta
that evening, which note should have been
despatched already, to relieve her mind of
the distress which must have followed upon the premature announcement of his

death. The last three months had wrought
a material change in Augusta's outward circumstances. Mr. Stuart, in his old age, had
taken a commission in the army. Tudor
Hall had been wasted and made a ruin
in the storm of war which had swept over
the fairest portions of Virginia; the young
lady's own property had been swept away
by the same devastating influences, and she
was at present residing with Miss Stuart,
in one of the northern counties of Kentucky, on the border-line between that
State and Virginia. Strange as it may
seem to the reader, when coupled with Mr.
James's previous generous declaration, the
loss of his bride's fortune had proved to
him a serious disappointment; he had secretly counted upon it to remove the cares
and straitnesses which always, more or less,
fall to the lot of the tyro in his early
years in his over-crowded profession; for,
whatever may be his talents, he must first
make them known to be appreciated, and
to not one in a thousand does the rare
opportunity offer to do this in the outset.

Mr. Leeson was too thoroughly practical to despise the generous dower which he was to receive with the hand of his affianced; and it may, after all, be questioned if this property did not weigh at the time in his rejection of Miss Bennet. True, the young couple had quarrelled, — a lover's quarrel, which chance might easily have reconciled; but Augusta, with her love and wealth, came between them. James was nothing loath to be won, as we saw, a few pages back; but his first ·thought in the matter was awakened by the evident partiality of his cousin.

"I must write to Augusta," he thought, "if my fingers are steady enough to hold a pen. It is uncertain if the letter will reach her; but I shall at least have fulfilled my part."

Unconsciously to himself, Mr. Leeson's closing remark showed which way his thoughts were drifting. It was not of his betrothed's comfort and ease that he thought, but of the duty devolving upon his side of the matter. Could that high-spirited young lady have guessed at the wandering state of mind from which emanated the few irregularly-traced lines which her lover now proceeded to pencil, with what blinding tears of mortification and anger would she have flung the letter beneath her feet!

To one other James Leeson's thoughts turned. Though not the most dutiful of sons, he could but regret the shock which this announcement of his demise must give his mother. He had not heard from her since the day on which he had left Bowling Green, and, of course, had no information of the unpleasant circumstances which had afterwards transpired. Little, indeed, did he dream that she could be in the same neighborhood with himself, breathing the same air; or that, in the smoke and din of that yesterday's battle, the officer who had twice drawn his unsteady aim, conspicuous for the gallantry with which he led on charge after charge, was his brother, Frederick! Could it be that a mother's prayer in one of those houses hard by unnerved his hand, and turned aside his bullet?

CHAPTER XLIII.

THE ESTRANGED LOVERS.

IT was a mutually-embarrassing meeting which the morning held in store for the alienated lovers. The gentleman reclining in his easy-chair, still pale with the languor of convalescence, presented an unusually interesting appearance, as he rose and took the hand of his visitor, with a few words of thanks for her kindness, of which he could not affect to be ignorant. His usual flow of words seemed quite to have deserted him; he fulfilled his part awkwardly, with an embarrassment as new to himself as it was secretly acceptable to the lady before him. She knew nothing of his engagement with his cousin. The story, though the property of the servants in the family, had by some uncommon good fortune been confined to the bounds of Wheatley Place, and she saw in his agitation only the reflection of her own, — the pleasure of meeting mingled with the pain of the new circumstances which environed them both. She had given to him a sister's care in these weeks of helplessness, and had not hesitated to share with his nurse in her vigils at his pillow; but to give back her old trust and the promise of her hand to a man who stood on the side stained with her parents' blood, was, of course, not to be thought of. She would gladly have refused even this interview, and the few more which might follow while they should continue under the same roof; but a voice whispered they might never meet again. The next battle-field might receive the misguided young man as a victim to the fate from which the care of friends had now snatched him.

"You owe me no thanks, Mr. Leeson," she said, struggling to regain her composure, as she took her seat. "You were wounded — dying, I at first thought — on that lonely field. It was but an act of charity, such as I hope would have been given to a stranger, to take you in."

"You have met with a great loss," said James. "Mrs. Anson told me."

"Yes; my dear father. He fell a sacrifice for his country. After my mother's death, he felt that he had a debt to pay. I little dreamed that he would fall in his first battle."

"These are dark days," observed Major Leeson, slightly at a loss how to offer consolation. "Many homes are already broken up, and the end does not look to me to be very near."

Jane looked at him earnestly. Was he already wavering in his heart over the choice he had taken?

"The end will not come till the South returns," she said. "Though all that I have is gone, yet, for the sake of those who must still suffer, I can pray that God will speed that blessed time."

"We shall never return," said Mr. Leeson; "it is a woman's thought to dream of it."

"You still believe that the purposes for which this struggle was opened will be carried out?"

"I do; I cannot doubt their success."

"God will not permit it," said Jane, fervently. "No such beginnings as these are prospered. You may not have seen, as I have, the desolated homes, the smoking ruins, the helpless families turned out to starve. What had my father done? Nothing; yet they burned his house, and turned my mother out to her death in the chill night."

"The fruits of civil war," said Mr. Leeson, gently. "They are reproduced in the heat and passion of such struggles in every country. Wait till you see some county or village of our poor Kentucky fall under Union rule, and you will see the same. Civil war is merciless!"

"You began it," said Jane, sorrowfully. "Where is the Union man who first put a torch to his neighbor's house?"

"You women feel rather than reason," said James, with a faint smile. "But what can you tell me of my family, Miss Bennet? I have not heard from my mother since I took my commission."

"I do not know what to tell you," said the young lady, hesitating, and glancing at his pallid face. "It is nearly eight weeks since I left Rossenville."

"My mother was then in her usual health?" asked James, startled at her hesitation.

"She was feeble, but not worse than she had been for some time."

Miss Bennet was keeping back a secret. Mr. Leeson noticed it with an uneasy perception of the fact.

"You have some unpleasant news for me," he said. "You need not hesitate. I think I can bear it."

"The worst is better than suspense," said Miss Bennet, wisely concluding it best to keep back a part.

"You are not aware that your brother,

Frederick, has taken a commission in the Union army?"

"I can scarcely say that I am surprised," said James, thoughtfully. "So that is your news? Can you tell me anything of his present whereabouts?"

"He was in the late battle."

James shuddered. "How fortunate we were kept apart!"

"I dare not stay longer," said Jane, rising. "I see you are growing wearied. I will come again to-morrow, if you like, or send in a book. Are you able to read?"

Mr. Leeson was not sure that his head would yet bear the application of steady thought; he made some demur to his visitor's departure; but Jane promised another visit, and hastily took her leave.

CHAPTER XLIV.

AN UNEXPECTED MEETING.

IT was a delicate task to break to Mr. Leeson the unsuspected fact of his mother's close proximity, and the more that the circumstances of both mother and son interposed to any immediate meeting. Mrs. Leeson had been removed to Belmont by easy stages, and had been taken to her chamber on her arrival, with very little prospect of again leaving it for any other change than to that narrow bed which awaits us each at some near or distant day. She was herself fully aware of her dangerous condition, and among the unquiet thoughts which pressed upon her mind came oftenest the image of the young daughter about to be left to the doubtful protection of her two

brothers. Frederick, she well knew, would
guard this charge as sacredly as his honor;
but his part was now in the foremost rank
of peril; beside the unfitness of a man to
preside over the destinies of a young girl,
his daily life lay in camps. Was there no
one of her own sex to whom she could commit her? If Frederick and Augusta had
married, Mrs. Leeson's dying pillow, despite
its still lingering thorns, must have been
crowned with content; but the perverse
girl had chosen to throw away from her a
true heart for one whose fickleness she
might yet know. Millicent was kind; her
aunt had grown to lean upon her in these
long weeks of feebleness and suffering with
an affection little short of that with which
she regarded her own family; but a poor
governess, setting aside the girl's still extreme youth, could be no fit guardian for
Adéle.

There was no friend left but Miss Stuart
to be consulted in this anxious hour, and,
quite ignorant of this lady's change of for-

tune in the long silence which had come
between them, Mrs. Leeson directed Millicent to pen a short letter to Tudor Hall,
stating in a few words the circumstances
which had lately transpired, describing her
present feeble state, and expressing a fervent desire to see her, as the last favor
which remained to be granted her in life.
Millicent dropped a tear upon it as she folded it. She knew that her aunt had grown
much worse since her journey; but she
hoped that with rest and quiet she might
again revive. Days went by, and the letter
received no answer. The battle of Belmont
took place. Mrs. Leeson passed through
the excitements of that terrible day alive,
and quite unconscious in its gray nightfall
that her son, for whom her prayers momen-
tarily ascended, was being borne past her
house to an adjacent dwelling. She knew
of Frederick's safety,— he had taken care to
send her a hasty message; but, though she
feared, she had still no assurance of James's
presence upon the field. Miss Bennet, who

had encountered Adéle once or twice in
the village street, came twice or thrice to
her sick-room; but her visits gave her little
pleasure; they brought painful associations
of the one event which might have turned
otherwise, and the girl's loneliness and or-
phanhood, strange as it may seem, brought.
up a painful picture of the future near at
hand for her child.   Sick pillows, where
the dying soul has yet much to learn of God,
are ever fruitful in morbid thoughts.

It was not until the morning after Major
Leeson had announced himself able to descend from his chamber, and had actually
got down to the bleak, frost-stripped garden to take in the strong, out-of-door air,
that Miss Bennet thought proper to com-
municate to him the unpleasant news which
had slumbered so long in her possession.
Wheatley Place, the home in which he had
been reared, and around which all his early
associations clung, was now a heap of black
ruins, and his mother, driven out on that
dark night for her life, was lying seriously

ill in one of these village houses, whose roofs rose in distinct view of his window.

"It was scarcely kind to keep me in ignorance," observed Major Leeson, whose second thought was that these facts should have been told before.

"It has spared you anxiety," said Jane, "which has been everything in your weak state."

Perhaps it had. He was feeling strong now. Two days at farthest, he had secretly decided, should see him on his way to rejoin his command. He would visit his mother; she could not refuse to see him, however little of satisfaction the interview might hold for either. Another reflection struck him, perhaps connected with this by some subtile train of association as he glanced at his patient nurse. He had acted foolishly in one important matter of his life, and he distinctly saw it. His acceptance of his cousin's preference had been unwise. It was Jane, and Jane only, whom he had really loved. Was there any possibility of retracing this step? Could Frederick be won over to accept the dowerless hand which, in the hour of prosperity, had been refused him? No, no! He knew that all this matter was at an end; he had made his election, and it must remain. It is a hard matter to accept an unloved wife. Mr. James Leeson, in the presence of the object of his secret choice, acknowledged this fact.

"You are wearied," said Jane, arranging the pillows of the lounge, and turning her eyes as she did so from the sunset skies, glowing with light clouds of crimson and gold, to the face of the invalid. "I fear my news has affected you unpleasantly. Mrs. Leeson is not by any means hopelessly ill; she has been much excited by the late battle, and a degree of weakness, of course, follows; but I think she will shortly rally."

"I was considering my own plans," said James, concisely. "I expect to be able to travel in a couple of days."

Jane's eyes dropped. The announcement

could not be said to take her by surprise;
yet all unpleasant tidings are in their nature sudden.

"There are many matters which I regret," said James, taking his companion's
hand, quite carried out of himself by the
sight of her emotion.

The door opened opposite; a lady wearing a travelling cloak, but otherwise hab-
ited in deep mourning, crossed the threshold,
Mr. Leeson, whose face turned toward her,
recognized Augusta. He dropped the hand
of the lady at his side, with a guilty glow
upon his face, and half rose to receive her.
Miss Bennet turned round, and, recovering
her self-possession with admirable quickness,
rose and went toward her.

Augusta stood like one who had received
a painful shock, her color wavering, her
eyes bright. She could not be blind to the
tableau her quick glance recalled. Her keen
jealously gave it a true interpretation.

"You did not get my note?" she asked,
hurriedly, addressing Mr. Leeson.

His eyes turned to the table upon which it was lying unopened. It had been taken up by Mrs. Anson while he was below in the garden, and had escaped his notice on his entrance.

CHAPTER XLV.

MISS BENNET was quite unaware of any cause for embarrassment in this unexpected meeting. Augusta's first sentence as she took the chair which the young lady placed for her explained her sudden appearance.

"We arrived an hour ago," she said. "Miss Stuart was too wearied with her journey to see you this evening. I left her in your mother's chamber."

"Until a few moments ago," said Major Leeson, "I had no suspicions of my mother's close neighborhood. These kind friends who have nursed me through my sickness thought best to keep back the knowledge until I should be able to leave my room."

383

"You have had a long confinement," observed Augusta, bestowing a look upon his nurse.

"I had forgotten to inquire for Colonel Stuart," said Major Leeson, glancing at her mourning dress, which had attracted his attention upon her appearance.

"You have not received our letters then?" Augusta looked surprised. "You are not aware of his death? He fell in a late skirmish."

"I was not aware of it," said Major Leeson, much shocked. "Your letters have all missed me. I have not heard from you directly since we parted."

Mrs. Anson knocked at the door. She held a letter for Miss Bennet. Jane went out.

An awkward pause fell between the two who were left together. James felt the wrong which he had been secretly doing his betrothed in his thoughts. Augusta was ill-pleased with the established presence of her lover's old *fiancée* in his sick-chamber, not to speak of graver anxieties which would intrude upon her, strive as she might to thrust them out.

"This visit is an unexpected pleasure, Augusta," said Mr. Leeson, penetrating her thoughts. "I had little hope of seeing you. In a couple of days I look forward to setting out to join my command."

"A letter from your mother brought us here," returned Augusta. "She was anxious to see Miss Stuart. I regret to tell you she is very ill."

He had guessed as much, carefully guarded as Jane's communication had been.

Augusta drew his attention to the gathering twilight, and rose to leave him. Her short call had proved unsatisfactory to both.

"When shall I see you again?" he asked, retaining her hand. She hesitated.

"I shall visit my mother to-morrow," he said, — "with her permission. May I ask of you the favor to obtain it?"

"She is by this time aware of your presence here," replied Augusta. "No doubt

Miss Stuart has told her. You need not hesitate to present yourself."

. "I shall come in at an early hour," said James, dropping her hand. She said her adieu quietly, and stepped out.

A new subject had come up for reflection as Mr. James reclined back on his pillows on the lounge. Augusta's lonely and orphaned condition required the fulfilment of his engagement. Her guardian and protector gone, her fortune wasted, he could not be blind to the only honorable course which opened before him. A few months before, a few weeks even, how gladly would he have taken upon himself these obligations!

Jane came back with a shadow of unusual thought upon her face. She took her seat at a little distance from the sofa, where the gathering dusk hid the gloom of her face.

James remembered the application of which Mrs. Anson had spoken, and guessed at the cause of her silence. "I hope your letter contains no ill news, Miss Bennet," he said, rousing himself to speak.

"On the contrary," said Jane, calmly. "It is a favorable answer to my application to be received as an assistant in a hospital. I shall set out on my journey to-morrow."

"So soon!" Yet it was best; he must bring back his truant thoughts, and fix them where his duty no less than his happiness required that they should henceforth rest.

Major Leeson's visit to her mother took place at an hour not far from noon on the following day. Mrs. Leeson received him in her chamber, which, indeed, she had not left since the evening of her arrival. Prepared as he was for a great change in her appearance, the sight of her wan face and silvered hair affected him unpleasantly; he sat down by her bedside wholly unable to frame the words which had risen to his lips at his entrance. Obedient to a sign from her aunt, Millicent had gone out. Adéle was not present. Miss Stuart and Augusta purposely absented themselves from this interview.

"You find me very ill, my son," said Mrs.

Leeson, withdrawing her eyes with a shudder from the distinctive uniform which, though stained and defaced on the field of Belmont, James had been obliged to resume in the absence of his servant with his other wearing apparel. "I feel that the close of these troublous days for me is near at hand."

"I trust you will grow better with rest," said her son. "Low spirits are always an accompaniment to a sick pillow."

"I am anxious for Adéle," resumed his mother, without heeding his reply. "Miss Stuart has told me of her own impoverished circumstances. I hoped to have given my daughter to her charge. The fortunes of life are uncertain. Yours and Frederick's, in these gloomy times, doubly so."

"I will provide for her," said Major Leeson, speaking with the earnestness of a promise in his voice. "Should the worst come, my dear mother, — which I cannot anticipate, — assure yourself that you are not leaving her alone."

"If you and Frederick could be recon-ciled," said his mother, wistfully; "but that is impossible! Oh, James, is it too late to leave the unrighteous cause which you have taken up, and which my dying eyes see can never be prospered?"

"I have no desire to quit it, mother." Major Leeson's voice was softened, but firm.

"You are about to marry Augusta?"

Major Leeson drew back a little at the abruptness of the question. "We are be-trothed, mother," he answered.

"You have done Frederick a grievous wrong, James," said his mother. "Your injustice will never be forgiven."

"We are all the creatures of circum-stance, more or less," returned Major. Lee-son; he did not add how heartily he wished it in his power to recall his part in these transactions.

"You have changed much, James," said Mrs. Leeson, attentively regarding him. "There are lines upon your forehead which were not there when you left us, and the old expression of your face is gone."

"I have not been living a holiday life in these last months, mother," answered Major Leeson, trying to force a smile. "We soldiers in camps taste few of the comforts of civilized homes."

"A poor evasion," said his mother, languidly returning his smile. "You begin to feel, James, that the cause you have entered upon is a perilous one."

"Far from it, mother; but let us close the subject if you please. I have chosen my politics; Frederick has chosen his."

"I shall see you again?" she asked, as, noticing the weariness which was creeping over her, he shortly rose to go. He murmured an assent, and went out.

CHAPTER XLVI.

MAJOR LEESON'S DEPARTURE.

MAJOR LEESON reached his own door just in time to hand Miss Bennet into the carriage which was waiting to receive her. It was better, this public parting, than the more dangerous adieu of a sick-chamber. Major Leeson involuntarily clasped the hand he was about to relinquish, and forced back the words which rose to his lips. He thought of the long night-watches, of the kind hours doled out to his weariness and weakness, and memory went back to the happy days at Rossenville, which were never to come again.

"He has chosen," thought Jane, glancing at the uniform which must now always be regarded by her with abhorrence. Regrets

391

are too late for us both, and with a fervent "God bless you!" in place of any colder term of adieu, she settled herself in her seat, and turned away her face.

Both were about to part for action, the greatest blessing in such shadowed hours, — the one for the field of strife and carnage, where life lies at the mercy of the whistling bullet and the whirring shell; the other, for those after-scenes, which are scarcely less mournful, and, unlike the field of battle, unenlivened by strains of music, or the excitement of triumphant charges.

An hour later Augusta came with Miss Stuart to pay Mr. Leeson a morning visit in his sick-chamber, and he was struck for the first time with the change in her deportment toward him. Could it be that she resented Miss Bennet's attendance upon him in these past weeks? It was very evident that she did. A glow of resentment flushed his cheek at these unworthy suspicions; he forgot for the moment how fully he had merited them.

The day but one following he had settled upon for his departure. There was little time to waste, and he seized upon the first opportunity of opening his plans to his betrothed.

Augusta listened to his proposals for their immediate marriage in a silence which boded ominously for their success. Perhaps she saw the cold impulse of duty, rather than of affection, which lay under it; certainly her sight, quickened by jealousy, had caught a distinct view of her lover's position. She could not forget the glow of guilt upon his face when she had surprised him after their long separation in the act of holding Jane Bennet's hand, and, tender and guarded as was his deportment toward her in the few hours which had passed since their meeting, she missed out of it a life, a vitality, which the old happy days had held.

Mr. James Leeson's fickle attachment to herself had quite evaporated with the loss of her fortune. It remained to be seen if her pride could consent to give him up.

Strange that this same motive which had actuated Frederick's suit for her hand should have secretly swayed his brother!

"I cannot consent to marry you at present, James," she said, quietly settling the subject. "So suddenly upon my guardian's death, it is quite impossible."

Major Leeson remonstrated. "The peculiar circumstances of the times, Augusta," he urged, "are a sufficient reason for this step. I shall feel more at ease in the dangers and exposures of the field to know that you are my wife, and that in case I should fall your future is provided for as far as any earthly means of mine can provide for."

If he had kept out the closing sentence! Augusta saw distinctly the cold lines of duty.

"My mind is settled upon the matter," she answered, coldly. "I shall not marry until I lay by my mourning for Mr. Stuart."

The subject was closed; Major Leeson said no more. Early in the morning he took his departure, after a sorrowful leave-taking of his mother and sister.

Augusta was not present; he met her in the hall as he came down. She gave him her hand. The icy coldness of her fingers struck him through her glove. " You will write to me ?" he said, in a low voice. " Augusta, what has come between us ?"

Millicent stepped into the hall from her morning walk. Both started, discomposed at sight of her. She held a letter in her hand, her face radiant with pleasure as she passed them.

" Adieu, Major Leeson," said Augusta, drawing away her fingers. "I hope you will be preserved safely through all that lies before you." She moved away, the folds of her light dress disappearing through the opposite door.

He looked after her with a sigh, and stepped out to mount his horse. He heard a sash raised, and looked up to see a face framed at the window. It should have been Augusta's. No, it was Adéle's. Tears were pouring over the child's face as she waved her farewell. Major Leeson returned it in silence. A mournful foreboding pressed upon him; he felt that he might never return.

"I dare not look backward," he thought, as he gave the rein to his horse. "Forward, forward, henceforth."

"Frederick is coming, aunt," whispered Millicent, bending over Mrs. Leeson's pillow. "He has a short furlough, and will spend two days with us. From the date of his letter, we may expect him to-morrow."

"You do indeed bring me good news, Millicent," said Mrs. Leeson, turning her languid face toward her with a reviving gleam of joy. "Just now it is sorely needed."

CHAPTER XLVII.

THE BATTLE OF MILL SPRINGS.

IT was the morning of the 19th of January, the day on which the disastrous battle of Mill Springs befell the Confederates, and turned the tide of their power in Kentucky. It was a dark morning, made chill with showers of drizzling rain. The contest opened at day-dawn, and was kept up until the shadows of night closed around the beaten army in their intrenchments. Foremost among those who, with a bravery worthy of a better cause, made stand after stand against the victorious army pouring upon them was Major James Leeson, rallying his men in the face of death, and fighting himself hand to hand—in many instances, side by side — with several of his old neigh-

bors. Close at his elbow, Captain Rawdon
levelled his musket at an officer not many
paces from them, whose familiar figure his
quick hate had recognized, and just at that
instant a passing ball buried itself in his
brain, and sent him headlong to the earth.
The struggle at this point now raged with
the utmost fury; friend contended with
friend, neighbor with neighbor; old feuds
were remembered, and late bitternesses found
their hour of requital.

"If poor Bennet could have lived to join
in this day," murmured Frederick Leeson,
as, emerging for an instant from the smoke
and dust of battle, he mounted a rising
knoll from which he could plainly see the
far-retreating columns of the enemy pressed
sullenly back at the point of the bayonet,
"with what zest he would have repaid his
wrongs!" Even as his lips framed the
words, a stray Minie ball from one of the
little group of stragglers still debating the
ground pierced his side, and he fell back,
with the warm blood gushing forth, just in

the edge of the wood. His comrades pressed on. They had no time to give to a wounded man, whose very fall was perhaps unheeded, though he had been a moment before the most conspicuous among them, such is the haste and excitement of pursuit, and Frederick laid his head wearily back on the wet ground, the drooping branches and low shrubs almost touching his forehead, while the tramp of steeds, the ringing of footsteps, the confusion of shouts, and the rattle of musketry died off in the distance.

It was a cold bed to rest upon, with a dozen stark forms lying around him, and two or three, yet conscious, sending up dismal groans as they lay parched with thirst, and groaning in the agony of their wounds.

It could not be far from high noon, though the sky was still overcast with the thick, flying clouds, from which now and then a fast pattering of drops descended on the dry leaves beneath. Frederick made an effort to draw out his watch; but his hand fell again nerveless by his side. Would they never come back? Must he die here, surrounded by these ghastly sights, with the chill rain dropping from overhead, and no gentle ear at hand to catch his parting words, to bear them to the dear ones whose nearness to his heart he had never so fully felt before? A hot heat and parching thirst began to creep over him; wild, fever-colored fancies grew to assume shapes in his brain; a drowsy, sinking sensation followed; he raised himself feebly, struggled to his elbow to send one last glance down through the naked vista of woods, and fell back exhausted and fainting on the wet ground.

When Frederick Leeson revived, he found himself lying on a bed in what seemed to be a poor log-house, with two or three figures flitting around him.

The nature of his wound, with the long hours of exposure which had followed, had brought on a severe attack of fever, and a degree of light-headedness which made him but partially conscious to surrounding objects. He believed himself to be in some out-of-the-way chamber at Wheatley Place after the first bewildered stare around his new quarters, and recognized one of the women who appeared at his bedside as his slave, Susan. He could not remember in his clouded state that Wheatley Place existed now only as a mass of ruins, or that his slave, Susan, had months before made good her escape, with her infant babe, from his ownership. By and by these misty fancies cleared; the dull pain ceased to girdle his temple; the burning heat which coursed through his veins subsided, and a long, refreshing sleep stole over his tired frame, from which he awoke in the full possession of his senses.

In one point Frederick had certainly not been deceived; it was his former slave, Susan, who watched at his bedside. The girl betrayed no fear. It might be that she knew her master's helpless condition to be for the time her sufficient safeguard, or it might be that in this lonely spot she knew it to be out of his power to put into action any immediate plans for her return into bondage.

Frederick was deeply surprised at the meeting; but it did not excite the emotions which must have agitated him at an earlier day. He knew that he owed his life to the care of these kind people, and he was not a man to overlook such an obligation, though rendered in part by one of his own fugitive slaves. He lay awake, considering the matter with much attention, and bestowing more than one thoughtful glance on the impassive face before him.

"How long have I been lying here?" was his first question.

"Nearly two weeks, sir," said the girl, without raising her eyes from her lap, where they seemed attentively riveted.

"So long! Ah, yes, I remember. How did the battle turn? When I fell, the enemy were in full retreat."

"It went on your side, sir. General Zollicoffer was killed, and many other officers. It was a total rout for his army."

"That is good news!" Frederick's face lighted up with a glow of satisfaction. He lay silent for a few minutes, and then turned his attention again to the figure at his bedside.

"Are you not afraid, Susan, that I shall claim you as my property, and take you back to your old life?"

A peculiar expression passed over the girl's face, a look which grew settled and hard.

"I will not go back alive, sir," she said, firmly. "I have made up my mind that the choice is easy between slavery and death."

"I will give you your liberty, Susan," said Mr. Leeson; "it shall be my first act, when my hand is strong enough to hold a pen, to make out your papers. It will be but a just return for the life which you have certainly preserved to me."

Perhaps Mr. Leeson overrated his gift. The girl had taken her freedom into her own hands, and it is difficult to see how on his sick-bed he could have effected her recapture; but his own view of the position of things was no doubt quite different. She was his property, liable at any moment to be rendered back by the law.

"I thank you, sir," said Susan, her low voice too tremulous to betray the character of her emotions. Ah, if this boon could have come earlier, of what inestimable value would she once have regarded it!

CHAPTER XLVIII.

MYSTERY OF SUSAN'S FLIGHT SOLVED.

THE long days of convalescence dragged
away slowly to Mr. Leeson in his narrow quarters. He longed to be in the field
with his comrades in arms, and fretted at
the irksome restraints which bound him to
a sick-pillow. But the long, lonely days of
illness were not wasted; they were fruitful
in many thoughts which had never visited
the strong, vigorous days of health. He
had stood too near the confines of the spirit
land in the last few weeks not to feel its
refining and purifying influences breathing
around him. The mighty struggle into
which he had been thrust began to take
broader bounds; he saw dimly a part of its
purposes, and his own past life of idleness

and leisure began to assume much of its true proportions. Not that his thoughts struck at the rotten groundwork of slavery. These convictions of the wickedness of pressing down human beings, with souls like our own, as beasts of burden, were yet in the future; but the soil was prepared, and the work begun. One question which had often perplexed him recurred now to his curiosity. By what means had Susan accomplished her flight from Wheatley Place? Friendless and alone, with her baby in her arms, she could never have carried out her journey. What secret friends, then, had aided her? He put the inquiry in a languid but earnest way.

"It is a matter which has been several times in my thoughts, Susan. I am anxious to know who of my neighborhood dared to give you assistance?"

"No one, sir." The woman's head dropped. "I walked on foot to the station. My baby sickened and died afterwards of her exposure in that cold, rainy night. I took the train. It was easy to pass myself off as a poor white woman travelling a few miles to see her friends."

Frederick was surprised. The railway had never occurred to him at all.

"How did you get the means?" he asked, finding his voice. "Borrowed of your mistress, I suppose?"

"No," said Susan, raising her head, a little proudly. "I had worked enough for mistress to deserve a trifle; but she always kept her money under lock and key."

"You had some friend, then, in my household?" observed Frederick.

Poor Susan's color changed; she had quite forgotten the suspicions which must follow upon her hasty denial. "I had but a trifle," she exclaimed, nervously; "it was not enough to carry me far. After I left the cars, I wandered about till I came to this lonely place, where I stopped to beg some food. My baby was then very sick. The woman took us in, and I have remained here ever since."

It was Millicent who had aided her in her flight. Frederick did not need to push further inquiries. Well, Wheatley Place was gone; the mortgage lay now upon the bare lands. Susan's flight had done him no great harm.

"These people you are with," he said, shortly, — "do they know your story?"

"I have kept it from them, sir; I dared not trust them; but I think they have suspected the truth."

"You are not aware," remarked Frederick, "that your old home has been burned up in the progress of this civil war, and that your mistress is now a fugitive, and lying ill at Belmont?"

"I was not, sir, indeed. Miss Adéle and Miss Millicent, are they with her?"

"They are, and old Dinah. The remainder of the servants, even Lizzie, have followed on your track."

"I should like to see the young ladies again," said Susan, thoughtfully, — "if I could be of any use. You promised to make out my papers, Mr. Frederick?"

"I will do so to-morrow," he answered. "Meanwhile, I have the impression that there are letters lying for me at Dalton. Can I induce Mr. Stedman to venture thither for them? I will pay him liberally."

"I think so," said Susan, rising with alacrity to step into the adjoining room.

"If he dares not face the risk," thought she, as a picture of the woodside country swarming with stragglers rose up before her, "I will myself attempt it. I feel sure I can get through."

CHAPTER XLIX

PARTING WORDS.

MR. LEESON'S letters brought him ill
news. He tore the first open eagerly,
recognizing the familiar handwriting, to read
a few tremulously-traced lines from Millicent, announcing that his mother was growing rapidly worse, and requesting him, if
possible, to visit her. The note was evidently penned in the hurry of a sick-room,
and the writer well-nigh exhausted by constant watching and care. The second was
from Adéle, and bore date a few days
prior to Millicent's. Their mother was very
feeble, she wrote; she seemed to be rapidly sinking. Would he come to see them?
She was sure it was possible for him to
get a furlough; she had just told Millicent

410

that James ought to be sent for. Frederick turned to the postmarks. Six days since Millicent's letter had been mailed! There was not an hour to lose. He must get up from his sick-bed, if he would see his mother once again in life.

His servant had made his appearance the day before, with his horse and baggage, through the instrumentality of Mr. Stedman, well satisfied to appearances to find his master still among the living. Excitement was beginning to supply the place of strength. Frederick knew that he would experience no difficulty in setting out. He distributed liberal presents to his kind entertainers, promised Susan an early message from him, and set out in the gray winter noon on his long ride to Belmont. A broad space of country, in all probability swarming with foes, was to be traversed. He had taken the precaution to don a suit of plain citizen's clothes, which his valise afforded.

Once before Frederick had set out on a

similar dismal occasion to what he then
believed to be his mother's death-bed. The
wide contrast between these days, though
not very far removed in point of space,
pressed upon him as he went on. Could
it be but eight short months before that
the railway train had whirled him through
the peaceful valleys of Virginia, his hand
yet warm from the clasp of his Cousin Augusta's, his betrothed wife, looking on to
years of idle affluence, with all that heart
could ask poured into his lap? To-day,
bound on the same mournful errand, he
found himself as another man; the pros-
pective of wealth, the every-day circle of
home comforts, gone, his property ravaged
and in ruins, his brother false, his betrothed
wife his no longer, the land lying all before him in the smoke and waste of civil
war; yet over all these elements a lighter
heart beat in his bosom than he had known
in the old idle days. His reason leaned
wonderingly to the truth that the soul is
greater than circumstances, and that sacri-

fice and trial are but the refining fires which bring out true manhood. It was a long, sad journey; but he bore up under it without rest or pause, and in the gray nightfall rode into the little village, and halted before the well-known house. His servant sprung down to assist him from his horse; for his wearied limbs refused to obey him, and, rejecting his further aid, Frederick rung the bell, and strained his eyes upward to catch the light which flickered out from the chamber above.

It was Augusta who faced him upon the threshold, drawing back with a change of color and clouded brow as she recognized the visitor.

"You are just in time, Mr. Leeson," she said, recollecting herself, and giving him her cold hand. "Your mother is living; she is conscious."

The words struck upon his heart. He dropped her hand, which he had taken with a movement scarcely less cold than her own, and came in pale and silent.

"You are ill, Mr. Leeson," said Millicent's voice behind them; her light step had tripped unheard down the staircase. "Your mother is awake. I will tell her you have come. But you must take some refreshment." His ghastly look struck her. She hurried out to get some wine.

Frederick took the glass from her hand. Augusta disappeared into the opposite room.

"You have come from a sick-bed?" she said, stopping to speak to him. "Only yesterday I saw your name in the list of the wounded of the battle of Mill Springs."

"There is no hope?" asked Frederick, reverting to his mother.

Millicent shook her head. "I will go up at once," she said. "She has been hourly expecting you. Thank God you have come!"

It was a mournful scene which the death-chamber presented, — a woman dying in what should have been the prime and vigor of her years.

A look of consciousness, of love, came

back in Mrs. Leeson's wan face as her favorite son bent over her pillow. If anything could have called her back to life, it would have been his presence.

Adéle crouched at the side of the bed, her face buried in her hands. Augusta and Miss Stuart were present. Millicent made a movement to withdraw. Frederick signed her to remain.

The dying woman's eyes wandered over the faces around her, passing from Augusta's to her son's. With the approach of death, her sight was beginning to grow strangely luminous. She saw the telltale shadows which rested on the young lady's face, and read their source.

."There is one burden upon my peace," she said, sending an earnest look toward her. "Augusta, my love, it would rejoice me to see you place your hand again in Frederick's. If I know his heart, I believe he stands ready to forgive the past."

"Not in that uniform," said Augusta, burying her face in her hands, with a quick shudder. "My country's enemies can never be friends of mine."

A scarcely-perceptible smile — shadowed and sad, as befitted a death-room — crossed Mr. Leeson's lips. His eyes wandered to a figure which had withdrawn itself to a distant window. He would not shock his mother's prejudice in her dying hour by telling her of his second and wiser choice. She would soon know all.

"Frederick," said his mother, looking up earnestly at him, "by the great love I have borne you, I pray you to forgive your brother. I cannot go in peace leaving you enemies."

"I have forgiven him," said Frederick, bending lower over her pillow. "I have myself just risen from a sick-bed, and have been close to the confines of that world where all things show in a clearer light. I forgave him then freely, as I hope myself to be forgiven, and taken to heaven, should I fall on one of these bloody fields."

His mother faintly pressed his hand. Her

eyes wandered out to the distant window.
"Millicent," she said,—"she has been kind
to us. I wish I could make some provi-
sion for her; she is alone in the world. Do
not forget it when I am gone."

Adéle's sobs were distinctly audible.
Frederick laid his disengaged hand gently
upon the child's head.

Mrs. Leeson's eyes closed softly, without an effort; her hand lay passive in her
son's; sight and hearing were gone; she
was sinking away. Miss Stuart drew near
the bed.

"Let me take her," she said, reaching
out her arms for Adéle. "Come, my love;
this is no place for you. Let me take you
to your own chamber. See, your brother
wishes it!"

27

CHAPTER L.

CONCLUSION.

THE funeral was over. All that was mortal of Mrs. Leeson had been laid away in an obscure grave in the village cemetery of Belmont; the mourning group had come back to the house. Millicent had retired at once to her chamber. Her heart was very sorrowful as she sat in the gray winter twilight trying to make real the great change which had come upon her lot. The cares and anxieties of the last long months were at an end. She was now free, alone, as she had been on the morning on which she set out from her New England home to take up this unseen burden of responsibility and toil. Only one little year! But she had lived years in these brief months in those experiences which are powerful to mature the heart and mind.

"I must go back," she thought, forcing down the sob from her lips. "It is hard to part from them,—Adéle and Frederick; but they need me no longer." She thought of poor Susan's words after her husband's sale,—"I wonder what God brought us into the world for!" The cry was upon her lips. Certainly the path which lay behind and before was rough and hard.

Some one knocked at the door. She started up to open it, thankful that the gathered twilight would conceal her tearful eyes and flushed cheeks. It was Mrs. Ayres, the lady of the house, who told her that Mr. Leeson wished to speak with her in the parlor. Doubtless it was upon the subject of his plans; his departure would take place at day-dawn upon the morrow; he had his excuse for intruding upon her grief.

"I will come down," she said, and going to the mirror, she put back her disordered hair, and bathed her flushed face.

Mr. Leeson was alone when she went down. Miss Stuart and Augusta gave him little of their countenance. They despised

the renegade Kentuckian, as they considered him, and not even the softening influences of a mutual sorrow could bring them
outside the bounds of a civil courtesy.

Frederick led his cousin to a seat. Neither
of them spoke for the first moment.

"I wish to learn something of your plans,
Millicent," Frederick said, at length. "I
leave here to-morrow, as you may be aware."

"I shall return to New England," said
Millicent, almost inaudibly. "It only remains
for me to bid you and Adéle good-by."

Frederick paused; he was standing at the
back of his cousin's chair, his face averted
from her observation. What he was about
to say seemed difficult of utterance.

"You know something of my history of
the last year, Millicent?" he began. "You
knew of my engagement to my cousin?"

"I heard of it at the time from the servants." Millicent drew a short breath. Was
the affair on the point of renewal?

"A heart which has been rejected by one
woman," returned Frederick, with a little
bitterness in his tone, "may not be regarded

as a fit offering by another. Millicent, if the future holds anything to repay this past to me, it must come from your hand."

She turned round toward him, her face glowing with agitated surprise.

"Do I understand you, Mr. Leeson? Can you forget the disparity between us? What would your mother have said?"

"You are my cousin, Millicent, — my poor mother's niece. If unacknowledged at first, your kindness to us all has at last brought home the relationship."

Was it a dream? Millicent thought so as she felt the warm clasp of his hand upon hers, and his lips on her forehead. The next words brought her back to recollection.

"Under the circumstances, it is best that our marriage should take place without delay. I wish to leave Adéle in your charge."

So soon after the burial! Millicent's face expressed disapproval. Frederick persisted. It would be better under the circumstances, and Millicent yielded.

It remained now to make the disclosure to Augusta and Miss Stuart. Frederick did so with a certain secret satisfaction. Both the ladies were surprised, Miss Stuart in a degree less than Augusta. She had seen something of the progress of events in the course of Frederick's former visits; but that his fancy for his sister's governess would culminate in a marriage went rather beyond her expectations. She ventured a few words of disapproval, which were becomingly met, and quietly answered.

"A few months ago," she said, "this step would have been far out of your thoughts, and the possibility of it as haughtily disdained by you as it can now be by us. This is one of the miserable consequences of the false stand you have taken. Oh, Frederick, if your father could have lived to see this day!"

"You would have found him on the side of the right," was Mr. Leeson's answer.

Miss Stuart had fulfilled her duty; she turned sadly away.

"I have a secret to tell you, Frederick," whispered Millicent, as she stole down to his side an hour later, while he sat alone in the parlor, his mind busied with the many thoughts of the future which might well press upon it; "it should have been told you this evening; but I forgot to speak;" and she went over hurriedly with the particulars of Susan's flight, bringing out her own co-operation.

Frederick smiled, — a smile which lingered pleasantly in the depths of his sober eyes and around his grave mouth, as he drew her agitated and blushing face gently round toward him. "I know all," he said, "and have only to thank you for the pleasure you have given me in your ingenuous simplicity. But, my dear child," he added, with a soberer brow, "were you not aware that you were laying yourself open to heavy penalties in aiding the flight of a slave?"

"I did not pause to think," said Millicent. "I saw only her distress, and the terrible fate she was trying to escape."

"A woman's answer," said Frederick, impressing a lover's kiss on the pure face. And in his heart he thought a woman's simple wisdom is sometimes the best.

We have little more to add. We can trace Frederick Leeson's path (under another name) through the three years which have passed since this record was closed; but over the fate of the other personages of our history a veil rests to us as well as to the reader. Whether James Leeson saw his error, and, like many of the misguided sons of his gallant State, came back to the old flag, and married Miss Bennet, or whether Augusta tardily accepted the fulfilment of his rashly-uttered vows, or whether, saddest of all suppositions, he fell on one of those blood-red fields, where half of the flower and chivalry of the South went down in their mad charges, are matters only for conjecture. Out of the storms of conflict and trial God brings peace, and so we need not doubt that in his own time and way he will make each individual experience of these bitter times fruitful of blessing, as well as raise our beloved country through these bloody scenes of purification to a higher estate than she has yet known.